Pony In My Pocket

Have you ever wanted something you cant have?

Shona Lawson

Shona Lawson

Pony In My Pocket

CONTENTS

CONTENTS

Note from Author

Hi, I hope you enjoy reading my book. I remember being that girl that wanted a pony when living in a central high rise flat in Scotland's capital where it wasn't possible. I achieved my hopes and dreams, and I hope you do too. I would love it if you could leave me a review on Amazon or Goodreads for my book to help me reach my next dream of getting my book out there. For reasons, that are too technical for me to understand, to do with algorithms and consumer patterns (or something like that), reviews make a huge difference. I would also really love to hear from any readers who would be happy to tell me their thoughts. It would be fab to learn about whether you think I should continue the book from where it stops, write more about the minimising telescope with new things getting minimised or about something new altogether. Enjoy!

Oh, and one last thing. Every time I get a five star rating an invisible fairy flies down and kisses my cheek - well in my head anyway.

Acknowledgements

Thanks to all the horses I have known, especially Cookie for being so perfect. Thanks to my daughter Lucy for inspiring me to do good stuff. Robbie, thanks for always telling me I can. Mum, thank you for making sure I got to know the importance of sitting on a horse most days. Poppy, thanks for bring all the balls back to me. Thanks to my friends for being goodies. Thanks to the baddies as its always more fun to have someone to prove wrong :)

One

Chapter 1

Pony in My Pocket

I enjoyed the poo. Moving pony poo was so much better than gymnastics, ballet, or ice skating. The horsey smell of sweet hay was an unmistakable aroma that filled my nostrils as soon as I walked through the big double gates to the yard. The gates clattered as they swung back and forth as cars passed through them. I spied a girl chasing a pony with a saddle and bridle through the car park area just beyond the gates and rushed to close the gates and pull the latch to make sure the pony didn't get onto the road.

The girl's brown hair bounced about as she chased down a little black pony, which had escaped from the riding arena. I glanced towards the arena; it was the place I went to in my mind when I was supposed to be focusing on boring things. I didn't need to check if the arena was still there, I just loved to see it welcoming me for more fun. The indoor arena was like a house originally built for giants but instead was a big empty space, with a floor of sand, for the ponies to be ridden around in. Originally painted green, but now the paint flecked off from the years of excited horse riders it had seen, and everyone was too busy having fun to do anything about it.

I just loved everything about being around ponies. I inhaled the atmosphere and felt that I had come to my happy place. I saw the girl catch up with the black pony and lead it back to the riding school. The truth was I would move a hundred million shovelfuls of poo to hang out with the horses at the riding school. It was so much better than normal school. It wasn't that I didn't like learning stuff. That was okay, but the girls in my class could be so catty. There were a couple of girls who always knew how to make me feel like I wished I wasn't there.

Bridgebrigg was a little village, hiding the riding school amongst the trees, making it feel like a secret place. The Scottish rain kept the grass growing up lush meaning the ponies had lovely fields to graze. Occasionally, I would see a for sale sign, amongst the rows of leafy trees and fantasise about what it would be like to live so near to the riding school. I imagined what it must be like for Holly to wake up in the morning and already be surrounded by acres of fields with the ponies in them.

Holly, the main instructor at the riding school, had exactly the job I wanted when I left school. Holly was very firm though, which I suppose came in handy with a stubborn pony or a helper who just wanted to brush and pet the ponies and laze around whenever she wasn't keeping her ever-watchful eye. I knew if I worked hard enough, I would get my monthly helper lesson so I was always eager to do whatever chores she gave me. I always got fumbled and mixed up around her through trying too hard to impress her. Holly casually flicked her hair behind her shoulders. I knew that I would somehow manage to say the wrong thing again today.

I saw that the girl had brought the black pony back to the indoor school and was prancing in a pretty trot effortlessly around the sides in a way that made me dream of the day I could do the same. I kept one eye on the pretty brown-haired girl and turned to face Holly.

Holly had a posh Edinburgh accent. Scotland was a strange place, that way - people could drive less than 20 miles and sound completely different.

"Hi, Holly, what jobs would you like me to do today?" I asked, looking at her sparkling smile.

"Okay Lilly, I've decided you're going to clean out the stables for the riding school ponies in the morning, then have your lunch and go to the indoor arena at half-past one and lead in some lessons. I want you to sweep the horse owners' barn up after that. Just don't get in the way of any of the owners while you're there."

"Thank you, Holly, that's great. I'll be invisible"

"Hey Holly, we're here for our jobs," said Erin. Erin's voice boomed as she bounded towards Holly, rushing so fast she almost crashed right into her.

Erin and Natasha always came running in together, with their packed lunches ready to find out their chores for the day. Even Erin and Natasha, the girls who made me miserable at school, couldn't put a damper on my riding school days.

Erin and Natasha dressed in clean new looking clothes, even in the yard. Proper horsey clothes, in nice crisp pinks and blues. The kind of clothes that looked, well, ironed. They came from the posh expensive estate not far from the school, with mothers dropping them off in cars that didn't have any squeaks or groans. Their little packed lunch boxes were this year's latest pony trend, unlike my boring plain pink one, that mum was so pleased with when she found as a bargain in the charity shop.

"Right girls, jobs are up on the whiteboard as usual. I've just given Lilly her jobs. Erin and Natasha, you're both doing the same as Lilly up until lunch, then you've both been booked into a lesson by your mums so you're only helping up until then. If you want to go back to helping after that you can clean the tack."

Erin and Natasha grinned and shared knowing smiles with each other. Erin's voice went right through me.

"I don't suppose Lilly will be managing a lesson this week," she smirked at Natasha. Natasha, the taller of the two girls, used her air of superiority to look down her nose at me. Holly ignored them and continued.

"Erin, I was thinking of moving you up into the same class as Natasha. You did well last week, and it means that you can start learning some jumping."

Erin squealed and grabbed Natasha's arm.

"Yesssssssss!"

Natasha smiled, and the girls started to bounce on the spot.

"Erin, you can ride Casper in your lesson today, and Natasha, you are on Sweetie. Take some time to enjoy grooming your ponies before your lessons if you like." Holly turned to me and said kindly, "Your helper's lesson is next week because that's nearly another month of helping."

Helper lessons were only half an hour, and you didn't get to pick your pony. Not that I minded—riding any pony was better than riding no pony at all. I usually got Smartie for my lesson, and I even forgave him when he was too lazy to want to go around the arena much. When Holly told me to smack him with the stick, I always hit my leg instead, hoping she wouldn't notice. I couldn't bear to smack him.

I knew what jobs I had been given, and didn't want to stay beside Natasha and Erin whispering their unkind remarks, to each other, and any of the other helpers that would turn up looking for jobs. My mood was high from learning I was getting to lead some ponies after lunch. I saw the girl from earlier still elegantly trotting around the school on her pretty pony and smiled at seeing someone having such a nice morning. The dirt track crunched below my feet as I walked. As I loaded my wheelbarrow with tools, my mind raced with all the things I should have said to Natasha and Erin.

This is the kind of moment that I wished I had something smart and witty to say to put Natasha in her place, but it never came in the heat of the moment. Maybe I was just too annoyed to be quick and clever right now, and not until much later, or I heard someone else with a smart quip I would think of what I *should* have said.

Two

Chapter 2

I went to find something else to muck out into, now my wheelbarrow was gone, and heard Natasha and Erin gossiping away. I prefer to muck out than to listen to all their meanness. There was something satisfying about cleaning a stable out, making it fresh and clean. Not that I ever felt that way about cleaning my bedroom.

Natasha and Erin always stuck together and never struggled with these smart witty things to say straight away at the right time. You know; these genius things like, "It's not your wheelbarrow Natasha, but it does smell like you," or, "Natasha, I had it first, like your boyfriend," but by then the moment passed.

Natasha and Erin started mucking out, both heaping the poo *into my* wheelbarrow while I was in the stable next door plopping the poo into the muck bucket I had found.

" Natasha, did you see she still has those riding boots with the holes on the sides?" said Erin.

I stiffened my jaw, raging.

Uncle Joe had bought me the boots two birthdays ago and I loved them. I remember the feeling of excitement rising in my stomach when I first saw them, and Uncle Joe popped them out from behind his back to show me. I didn't want to throw them out now all the stitching at the side was breaking. Mum had popped them in the bin when I was in bed once, but I sneaked them back out and kept them in my backpack for the stables at the weekend. I couldn't face going back to trainers again after having my own proper riding boots.

Uncle Joe had said he might get me a riding lesson for my birthday this year, so I didn't want him to know about the worn-out boots. I knew I couldn't have both. Taking early retirement since he couldn't tell when he would have a good day or bad day made it hard for him to commit to set timescales. There were days that Uncle Joe would look fine and days that he would find everything exhausting. Uncle Joe's health had changed and he couldnt always do everything that he wanted to do.

"My mum has booked me a block of ten riding lessons now, and she's hired me a pony for the riding school show on Wednesday night." said Erin "Are you coming to watch Natasha, or do you have a pony too?"

"I don't have one booked yet. I'll have to tell Dad when I get home. I have to remind him at least three times to do anything." replied Natasha.

"You're lucky he remembered to make your sandwiches then. I've sneaked a bag of apples in my bag. Let's give some to the ponies when Holly isn't looking." said Erin.

I blocked out the girls' chattering and enjoyed being in the moment of doing the stables. The clean straw that lay at my feet felt all soft underneath me, letting me know I had made a nice thick bed for the pony to come in and sleep on. I loved making their beds nice and fresh so that the ponies would have somewhere clean and dry to lie that night. I looked over to the corner where the big pink water bucket sat. I emptied it, cleaned and refilled the bucket with fresh water. It looked refreshing for any pony who wanted to dip their lips in and take a drink. The bits of hay and yucky stuff that had been floating in the water before I found it had been replaced with clean, pure clear water.

Natasha and Erin worked away for the morning in the same stable block as me. They talked about me and my broken riding boots as though I wasn't there, but neither of them said a word to me once they had taken away the wheelbarrow. I knew it was time to stop for lunch when the girls ran off. I wasn't going to ask them the time and my broken watch wasn't much help.

Lunch was always great at the riding school. I would sit on the grass at the top of the hill and eat my lunch while I watched the ponies in the fields grazing. The ones that weren't in the stables or getting ridden, anyway. I loved sitting on the long grass, getting my bum all wet if it had been raining, enjoying the calmness of the ponies grazing away, and chewing rhythmically. If I listened hard, I could hear them tear the grass from the ground and grind the grass down with their teeth.

"The smell of the horses doesn't put you off your lunch either, then? Mind if I join you?" said a girl as she came and sat next to me on the grass.

She brought such a pleasant vibe with her. I was happy she had decided to come and sit by me.

I smiled. "I just love being around the ponies. I get a lesson every month for helping out here on Saturdays," I told the girl.

She had beautiful long hair. It shone like a horse's coat when it was ready for the show ring. Her teeth were perfect and straight like an American film star's. The girl had long slim limbs, and surely if she were a horse, she would be a thoroughbred. She had the look of the kind of girl who knew how to do a good rising trot. Her boots were not ripped like mine but had seen a lot more action than the shiny new boots that Erin had. I wondered if they were hand me downs from a bigger sister or if she had gotten a lot of riding lessons. I could see the soft leather had moulded around her feet so that every scuff and mark had its own riding story to tell.

"Oh, I'm new here. I'm Kalila. My family just moved from down south to be back near Gran. Yeah, I love chilling here too. Sitting eating my lunch and watching the ponies." said the new girl.

I wondered if she was here for a riding lesson or as a helper. I guessed she was maybe lucky enough to have weekly riding lessons because she had the proper jodhpurs. I hoped she still wanted to be so chatty with me when she found out I was just a helper without all the fancy extra riding lessons.

"What's your name?" asked Kalila

"Lilly."

"Cool, Want a packet of cheese and onion? My mum always packs them, and I can't stand them."

"I can swap them for a banana?"

"Deal."

"It's nice having someone to eat my lunch with. The other helpers have lunch in the yard caravan, but I prefer being with the ponies. Ponies are nicer. Except maybe Zippy down there. He can bite you, sometimes."

"I've struggled to get to know anyone yet. Are the other girls okay?"

"I go to school with some of them as well and they don't like me. I prefer to be with Zippy anyway...he's less mouthy."

Kalila smiled. "Well, you can have lunch with me now if you like. I'll be here every Saturday. Is that the day you come down to help?"

"Yeah."

It was great to have a horsey friend. Now we could hang out and be helpers together and she could come to my house for tea and meet

Uncle Joe. When Natasha was being horrible I would have someone there for me. I was beginning to get what it would be like having a horsey friend all planned out in my head.

"I'd best go and get ready. I'm leading some of the horses in the beginners' lessons next. I'll see you here for lunch next Saturday if you're back. Nice to meet you, Kalila. Let me know if you need a hand finding anything here since you're just new." I said

"Thanks for having lunch with me. I'm sure we will bump into each other later" Kalila said.

I headed back to the riding arena over the lush grass looking at my feet and hoping Natasha and Erin didn't bump into her first, as she might prefer to hang out with them.

Three

Chapter 3

I loved getting to lead in the lessons. I would run around with one of the little kids on the back of a pony. I would put a lead rein on the pony's bit and make sure it didn't wander off with its rider until they learnt to hold the reins properly.

Holly was the best instructor ever and taught me a lot of cool stuff.

"Hi, you're early, Lilly. Can you manage to lead Pepper today? If you bring him in just now before the lessons start, I'll show you how to change stirrup lengths and then you will have learnt to do another job for me."

I dashed away to fetch Pepper. I loved learning new things about how to be helpful around ponies. When I came back Holly was tidying up the jumps in the corner, making sure all the jump wings were neatly put away. Holly stood taller than the jump wings that she moved effortlessly. Holly's height made her strong for dealing with even the naughtiest ponies. Her hair fell in curls around her shoulders, not from hours of being curled in irons but from not seeing a hairbrush in days. Holly's fair skin and hair made her look like a scruffy Rapunzel, but not one in a tower; more one that had woken up from sleeping out on a camping trip.

"Right, you did a great job of checking the girths last week. You just talk me through how to check a girth again and then I'll show you stirrups."

"I put my two fingers under the girth here and check how loose or tight it is. This one is a little loose for a rider to get on with and needs to go up."

I demonstrated to her by sliding two fingers under the girth near the pony's armpits to feel how loose it was and felt a little gap that told me it would slide as a rider was trying to climb on if I didn't put it up a few holes.

"Fab, Lilly, so show me what you do next."

I pushed the saddle flap up and struggled to get the buckle up to the next hole. I clumsily faffed about until I got it in. I could feel my tongue sticking out the side of my mouth with concentration so quickly pulled it back in.

"Okay, it's important you remember that. If the girth's not tight enough the saddle can slip round with the rider still on. Now to do the stirrup, it's the same type of buckle. It's important that we keep them the same length on both sides and do it nice and quickly if the rider is on board. You push the buckle up this way to pull it out the hole, then move the leather and put the rider's foot back in for them," said Holly as she talked me through it.

"Like this? I'm pushing up but it's quite stiff and hard to get out."

"Keep going. You'll get it. That's it; well done, Lilly."

I smiled.

"Next thing to learn will be how to do it for yourself when you're on the horse. We will cover that if you come early for your next helpers' lesson."

"Thanks, Holly."

"When Pepper's rider comes in, I want you to try and check the girth and change the stirrups for the rider, but you must call me if there are any problems with it, okay?"

"Yeah, sure."

I was so happy to be around the ponies that I forgot to be nervous around them, even when calling out in group lessons. It was so much easier than in class at school as everyone was too busy looking at the ponies to worry about me anyway. Part of the magic of ponies I enjoyed, I suppose, was how they could put me at ease. Something about the sweet tang of the horse sweat meant that every time I breathed in, I felt more carefree. Their casual acceptance of just knowing that I was a good person, just chilling and enjoying my company as they went about their business was so beautiful to me. I loved how they seemed to know I felt and had an undemanding presence. All my worries about school, Uncle Joe's health and Mum managing to pay all the bills just fell away when I was around the ponies so that I could just enjoy their company. My stresses dissolved until all I felt was acceptance and calm whether I was petting them, stroking them, or just sitting watching from across a field. When I got to help Holly in the lessons it meant extra close pony time and all the happy feelings meant that there was no room for anything else

I loved helping lead the pony in the lesson. I listened to Holly greet a little girl when she came in.

"Okay, so we have six horses in this lesson today. I thought you could ride Pepper. Do you like the idea of that, Robin? Lilly can take you and get you sorted on Pepper."

Robin jumped up and down and looked very excited as she rushed over to me, her little legs moving as fast as they could go to get her to Pepper.

"I love Pepper, Lilly. I can't wait to get on."

Robin was only little, but her mum always stayed in the viewing area rather than the main riding part as she didn't like to walk in the arena with her high heels on. Robin was really lucky that she always got a lesson every week. She was so cute and only five or six, but her mum had even got her a riding hat of her own. It was easy to enjoy leading Robin when her smile and bright twinkly eyes on arriving showed me that she loved her pony time just as much as I did.

"Okay, I'm glad we have each other again, Robin. Remember to hold on tight to the mane once we get you on. You climb up the mounting block and I'll help you up."

I checked the girth and once Robin was on, I changed her stirrups for her to the right length for her little legs with my tongue sticking out of the side of my mouth again.

"Look at me, Mum. I'm on Pepper again. Look!" she squealed.

Robin's joy was infectious. She was a lovely little kid. Robin's mum's lips stood out even from the distance, her bright red lipstick glistened, as she smiled at Robin and waved back.

"Well done, Robin. Now hold on tight and listen to Lilly and Holly."

I waited until Robin stopped waving at her mum and gently put her hands on Pepper's mane to encourage her to hold on and then I led her off. The lesson had properly started as Holly addressed all the riders at once.

"Okay, when you're on your pony, start walking it around the arena at large."

I knew what *at large* meant, it meant around the whole arena. I was pleased with all the new things I was learning.

"Lilly, what kind of pony is Pepper? I read about hairy ponies being called Shetlands in my pony magazine. Is she a Shetland?"

I was proud I knew the answer to this. "She's an Exmoor, Robin, but I can see why you might think she was a Shetland with her shaggy coat. Pepper is very cute, though."

I didn't let on it was something that Holly had only taught me a few weeks before. The best thing about leading was that I could give the ponies sneaky pets under their manes as I led them around. I would inhale deeply, trying to get as much of their sweet rich smell in as I could. The distinctive horse scent that came off the ponies and stuck to my clothes was so much nicer to sniff in than Robin's mum's perfume. The more natural perfumes that nature had to offer might have been rougher around the edges but they didn't hurt my nose.

Four

Chapter 4

When leading in the lesson was over, it was time to sweep out the barn. I checked the time on my watch—before I remembered it was still broken. It still had unicorns on it, so I wasn't taking it off.

I loved being trusted to work in the owners' barn. The owners' barn was where people who had their own private horses kept them. Nobody else was allowed to ride a privately owned pony and their owners could ride them every day if they wanted to, even if they didn't have a riding lesson booked in. It was the smartest block with all the horses with nice new-looking clean headcollars and rugs hung outside their stables. I could sneak loads of pets and cuddles to the horses that weren't out in the field and still in the owners' block during the day.

I grabbed the biggest sweeping brush from outside the block and headed in to start getting the whole barn swept out. There were loads of stables all the way down on each side of the stable block. There was straw and hay everywhere needing to be topped up.

I looked at the stable door and saw a stable name saying, *Barney*. I had seen Barney before. He was a big brown horse and did fancy competitions and his owner even had a horsebox to take him away in. It must be wonderful for Barney's owner. I started to sweep while

I dreamed of how it must be to be Barney's owner as I made my way down the stables, not missing any bits.

"Hey there, fancy seeing you here," came Kalila's voice.

"Oh, cool, are you mucking out in the owners' barn today? I'm getting to sweep," I told her. "It's fab that we've been put in the same block."

"Yeah," she called back.

"Oh, there's a pony still in there. You might want to start in another stable, so you don't get into trouble with Holly," I called. "I can show you the ropes if you like."

"Actually", said Kalila "This is Chintzy. She's mine. You wanna come in and help me brush her? I love seeing how shiny I can groom her."

"You have your very own pony all to yourself?"

"I've had Chintzy for a few years; we've kinda grown up together. We were in a livery yard before but when we moved my mum wanted me to be at a riding school where there were more kids to hang around with. I still go to Borrowstoun Academy and that's ages away."

"Oh, is that the posh school?"

"It's not posh when I'm there. If you come in, I'll let you brush Chintzy with me."

I couldn't believe my luck. "Yeah, I'd love to."

I went into the stable and bolted the door shut behind me. Chintzy was the most beautiful pony with a pretty face. She sparkled with her whiteness and had her thick tail so brushed out she looked like something out of a picture book.

"There's all my grooming kit over there. Help yourself."

I looked at all the brushes but there were so many I didn't know what one was for what and I didn't want to look stupid.

"Just pick up the dandy brush to start off with, and I'll do her mane."

Oh no. She wasn't going to want to be friends with me when she realised that I didn't know as much as Natasha and Erin about horses. I tried to figure out what to do. I wondered what even was a dandy brush and decided I had to make a decision or look even more foolish. I picked up a random brush.

"Hey, that's the body brush, grab the pink one beside it," Kalila said.

"Thanks," I told her. "I always wanted to brush and groom the horses, but I haven't talked my mum into getting me an *own a pony* day yet."

"That's okay, none of us knew until someone told us. Even the top show jumpers don't know everything."

OMG, she was amazing. Natasha would never admit she didn't know everything about horses and ponies, and she wasn't a top show jumper. She got riding lessons in the poles class and got to do the fun days at the riding school, but she wasn't a top show jumper yet.

"Chintzy is so beautiful. White horses are so striking."

"For some reason, white horses are always called grey horses," she said without any of the smugness that Natasha used when she knew something that I didn't.

"That's mad."

"That's what I thought when I found out."

"You're so lucky, to have such a lovely pony."

"Yeah, my mum thinks the more time I spend with a pony the less chance there is of being interested in boys or drugs; that's what she tells my gran, anyway."

"She's right. Who would want to hang out with boys when they could have a pony?" I laughed. Even if Andrew at school was nice and kind, I'd much rather have a pony like Chintzy than a boyfriend any day.

"There's a jumping night on Wednesday. You can come and watch if you like."

"I'd love that. I could ask Mum if I could come here straight after school. I could help you clean your stable."

"I like cleaning my stable and one of the instructors usually does it anyway. You can keep me company...or we can do it together. I have to rush from school to make it with it being a lot further away."

I wished Kalila went to my school and not the posh school in town. I didn't have many friends at school, and I wasn't allowed to Rebecca's house after school anymore. Not since my mum collected me from her house and Rebecca's mum had too many glasses of wine to hear the doorbell.

It was great having a new friend. I was just worried if she would still like me when she met Natasha and Erin and heard all the mean things that made everyone laugh about me. Maybe she would meet them and realise how much more they knew about ponies than me. Or how much better they could ride than me. Or how I didn't have the right gear. Ever noticed that when you worry about something it always turns up?

Natasha came breezing into the barn. "Lilly Four Eyes, you're not supposed to be in the horse owners' barn. You need to help Erin and me fork up the muck heap now."

"I'm in here to sweep the barn, Holly asked me to."

"OMG, and you're in one of the stables with one of the horses. I'm telling!"

Kalila spoke up, "I asked her to come and help me brush," said Kalila, "It's my pony."

"Why does she get to come and help you? You know she ate her own bogeys all through primary 3?"

Kalila turned to face Natasha. "Can you leave, please? This is the owners' barn, and no helpers are allowed."

"What about Lilly, then?" asked Natasha. Erin appeared behind Natasha wandering up to stand beside her.

"She's here as my friend, not as a riding school helper. I'd like you to go now as you're being unkind."

My mouth opened. I couldn't believe how cool and calm and collected my new friend was in getting rid of Natasha. My cheeks were warm with the embarrassment of what Natasha had told her, but Kalila mustn't have believed her.

Holly came into the barn at that point and saw Natasha and Erin.

"Hey girls, how's the sweeping up going on here? Not quite finished yet? Have you two come to give Lilly a hand?" She turned to Natasha and Erin.

Oh no, I was in so much trouble being in the stable and now nice Holly would be annoyed with me for skiving when I should be working. It was one of the most basic rules to never touch any of the privately-owned horses. I didn't want to lose her trust and then be put back to only being allowed to poo pick the fields and not be allowed around the horses. It had taken me months to build up to being allowed to sweep the owners' barn and lead the horses from when I started.

I was still thinking of what to say to be in the least amount of trouble when Kalila answered. "Hi Holly, I asked Lilly to come in and give me a hand with something."

"Okay, that's fine. Lilly can be here if she has an owner's permission. Glad to see you're already making friends here. What about Natasha and Erin?"

"I don't know them. I was just enjoying hanging out with Chintzy and Lilly. Can you not turn Chintzy out tomorrow morning for me? I want to come down and ride early."

"Sure, I'll stick some hay in and check her water till you get here. Come on girls, you know the rules. No helpers in the owners' barn unless they have a specific job."

Wow, Kalila was powerful. She could even tell Holly what to do, and she spoke to people so nicely.

"I love hanging out just chilling in here with Chintzy," Kalila told me.

I smiled.

"Want a shot of her mane brush? I want to get her all pretty for the show next weekend."

"That's amazing. I'd love to go to a show one day. Is that the pony gymkhana day? Some of the girls are going to hire a pony and join in. I want to do it one day. I thought it was Wednesday, though."

"You're welcome to come and watch. It's not the show here though. It's a special jumping one. I will be doing the fun one here on Wednesday but next weekend my mum's taking me to one off the yard in the horse lorry. You can come with me if you want. There's a spare seat in the horse lorry."

"I've never been in a horse lorry before. I'd love that."

I heard a lady walk up to the barn and I went quiet. She might be about to give me a row for being in the owners' barn or going to see her horse, but she walked straight up to Kalila's stable.

"Hi, Mum."

"Hi, chicken; see? You're making friends already."

"Yeah Mum, this is Lilly. I said she could come to the horse show with me next weekend."

I was shaking on the inside with excitement. Now I knew why Robin jumped up and down when it was time to get on her pony.

"Great. I'll bring extra packed lunch stuff along. We usually leave quite early for a show so if you're here for eight in the morning that would be ideal."

"Thank you so much. I can't wait."

"Right, it's time for you to come home, sweetheart, so finish up now."

I came out of Chintzy's stable and went back to sweeping the barn. I wondered what I would wear to the show. I was lost in my thoughts as I finished my sweeping, thinking of the show. I should have asked where it was as my mum would want to know that, but I felt nervous about going back over to speak to Kalila's mum. I was so content when Mum came to collect me from the stables that day.

"Mum, I made a new friend and she's really pretty. She has her own horse and everything."

"That's fab Lilly, another horsey friend. Does she ride well?"

"I didn't see her ride, but her own pony is called Chintzy, and she is going to ride her in a show next weekend. I can go with them to watch."

"At the yard? When? Do I know this friend's mum?"

I knew from my mum's pitch that my problems were beginning. Her voice always went higher when she was worrying.

"It's off the yard but it's okay. My friend's mum said I can go with them in the horse lorry. Kalila's mum seems lovely, but they have just moved here so I don't think you know them. You can come and meet her."

"So, you want to go away to a place, you don't know exactly where, with strangers? In a lorry with what carbon footprint on the environment? And what time will you be back?" Mum's voice got higher with her questions, which was as bad as a *No*.

I felt a sadness rise in my chest replacing the excitement that had been there before. My dreams of getting to enjoy a horsey day at a fancy show were slipping away.

"Can't you just speak to my friend's mum? Then she won't be a stranger."

"Got her phone number? Or do I just have so much time on my hands with working all hours that I could randomly walk around in circles in the town centre in the hope that I meet her?"

Damn. I should have thought of that and asked for her phone number. If I had been allowed a Snapchat or Facebook account none of this would have been a problem as I could have just looked her up that way. Or at least if I'd had my own phone...even much younger kids were allowed their own mobile normally. I'd have argued with Mum for hours if I had thought it would have made any difference. Instead, I stayed silent the rest of the drive home.

Five

Chapter 5

"I drew you this," said Rebecca. "I know that you really like ponies, so I thought you'd like it." I smiled at her. I always felt awkward getting the right words to say. Rebecca slid the picture over to me and I hid it under my workbook. "You'll have something to remember me by when I go to my new school."

I wished Rebecca hadn't reminded me she was leaving. It would be lonely without her, and I wouldn't have anyone to sit next to at lunch, now. I heard giggling and looked up.

"Right!" Mrs Brown shouted. "Erin, Natasha, too much chatter is going on from your table. I'm going to have to move some people around. Lilly, you go and sit in between them. Let's see if a nice sensible girl at the table can show them how to be a bit quieter."

My face went pink. I did not want to move and sit beside Erin and Natasha. I'd much rather have sat anywhere else; even at Kieran's table and he scribbles on everyone's jotters next to him thinking it's hilarious. I thought about pleading my case to stay at the table, but that would mean I'd have to speak up in front of the whole class and Mrs Brown would just make me move anyway. I grabbed my workbook and jotter, keeping Rebecca's picture under it as I moved over to the table.

Mrs Brown said, "Right Erin, you move along one seat, I want Lilly sitting in the middle of you pair. I can't hear myself think with all the noise you two girls make."

Erin complained. "Oh, does she have to sit here? We will be good."

Mrs Brown said, "That's enough, Erin, do as you are told and listen up. I have an exciting project to tell the whole class about."

When everyone was watching me move between tables, Erin tried to argue with the teacher.

Kieran took his chance to throw an eraser in my direction. It pinged off my arm and didn't hurt much, but I looked up at Mrs. Brown to see if she would sort it out. Erin had Mrs. Brown too distracted as she was arguing with her, and Kieran chuckled to himself.

"Right, so it's inventors' week next week, so we all need to make something that works. It can be a pencil holder or have moving parts, like maybe an egg timer. We've been collecting old cereal boxes and crepe paper in the box at the back of the class, but of course, you can use anything that you have at home so long as..."

"Aaaahhhhhhh!" the words escaped my mouth as a sharp pain came across my shins. Natasha had kicked me hard under the table and it smarted badly with the hard extra-thick sole she had on her shoe.

Mrs Brown looked over at my new table. "Are you starting up now too, Lilly? That's not like you."

I wanted Natasha to get a row from Mrs Brown and stop hitting me, but if I told tales Natasha and Erin would just take my schoolbag away from me after school and throw it in the river again. "Sorry, um..." I felt my face redden as I had to speak aloud in the classroom with the full class listening. I shifted in my seat uncomfortably, trying to get the words out in front of everyone. "I, er, sneezed. Sorry."

Mrs Brown said, "Okay, well sit quietly and listen, as there is a prize for this project, and I think we could all have a go at doing well."

Mrs Brown kept on talking and Erin whispered, "You're lucky you didn't do your tell tailing like a speccy grass. You better believe that they think it's a sneeze."

Mrs Brown looked over. "Is there still noise coming from this table? Are you all chattering now? Do you want me to give extra homework to the whole table?"

The whole class looked at our table. I looked down at my exercise book.

Natasha said, "Sorry Mrs Brown, Lilly was just trying to find her pencil, we will be quiet now."

Andrew and Brett looked at me furiously as though it was all my fault. Brett tore off the corner from a sheet of paper and made a little ball. He took aim and threw it at my head. I looked down.

Mrs Brown said, "We're all going to do some artwork now. Put your jotters away once you have taken a note of your science project, and I will be coming around with a water jar and some paints. I want the group leader from each table to come and get a brush for each person at the table."

Brett loved being the group leader. Mrs Brown always thought he was perfect, and I think Natasha did too. Brett returned with the paintbrushes and passed them around as Mrs Brown placed a water jar and some paints on the table. "Now I want everyone to draw a picture of their favourite animal, and work on your shading with the brush."

I loved art, and I couldn't wait to get started on painting a nice picture of Smartie. Pretty Smartie always had hugs and love for me, and she only bit me when she thought I was hiding a tasty carrot from her. Not like Zippy who bit anyone every chance he got.

Natasha said, "Typical, I have speccy you sitting between me and Erin so we can't talk because you are a goody-two-shoes. Now you're copying me." I looked over and saw that Natasha was painting a pony picture too. Natasha carried on, "Your pony has a wonky neck, and it looks like a giraffe."

I saw she had a point about my pony's neck. Maybe I could paint a bridle over the pony's head, so it didn't look so bad. I reached over to dip my brush in the water, but I misjudged and sent the water spilling all over the table, soaking Natasha's painting.

"Mrs Brown, Lilly ruined my picture because my pony was better than hers," Natasha yelled.

Mrs Brown came over and said, "Well they are both good ponies and look, they're nearly all finished. You go and put yours on the radiator to dry and you can finish off tomorrow."

Natasha came back from putting her painting on the radiator and told me, "I'm gonna sort you out on the way home once we are on the bus. You did that on purpose."

Andrew looked up, and said, "Why are you being so nasty to her? You all like the same things. You are all painting ponies 'cos you all like them. Why can't you just be nice to each other?"

Natasha always knew what to say straight away. "Because Lilly is stupid. She doesn't even get proper riding lessons so she can't ride like me and Erin. Anyway, her specs would fall off if she tried having a proper jumping lesson like us. She spoiled my painting because she is jealous."

Andrew replied, "You know your reasons for being mean make no sense, right?" and carried on with his picture.

I looked up at Andrew, grateful that he had said something. He seemed so grown up and kind. I'd have sat with him at lunchtime after Rebecca left for her new school but then everyone would say he was my boyfriend. When the bell went for the end of school, I took my time getting out of the classroom.

"Come on Lilly, you will miss the bus. Get a move on," said Rebecca.

"It's okay, Rebecca, you get your lift home with your mum. I want to take my time."

Rebecca said, "I'll walk you to the bus and wait if you're worried about Natasha and Erin."

The last time I had upset Natasha this much she sneaked up behind me on the bus and emptied her crisp packet out on my head. I smelt of ready salted for the rest of the day.

"No, that's okay, I'll walk rather than take the bus and avoid her. I'd rather walk through the fields and see the ponies on the way anyway. You get the lift with your mum, and I'll see you tomorrow. Let me know what you're making for the project, and I'll tell you my ideas."

Rebecca walked towards the classroom door which stood open with no teachers left in sight; they were probably outside chatting with each other.

She said, "Okay, don't let them get you down. You don't want to be friends with wallopers like that anyway. Natasha is just all mouthy 'cos she thinks you won't smack her back. You should try it sometime, so she leaves you alone."

I pictured in my head me reaching out and slapping Natasha's cheeky face and wondering how it would feel to do it in reality. I smiled for the first time that afternoon. I headed off on the paths across the fields that would take me to Uncle Joe's. I saw Andrew walking with his mum and his mum called out, "Lilly, aren't you going to the after-school club? I thought your mum worked late on Mondays."

"Yeah, she lets me walk to Uncle Joe's instead now."

Andrew looked embarrassed by his nosy mum as she carried on. "Oh, that's great. Not seen Joe in ages, tell him to give me a ring sometime. Does he still have Bessie?"

I kept walking in the same direction as her but knew she would head off when the path split a few metres away.

"Yeah, he does, and I will do," I said as I carried on towards Uncle Joe's.

I felt great knowing school was done for the day and looked forward to seeing Uncle Joe. He would tell me, "You are the kid that I never had." He would take me on walks, make stuff with me, always had the latest computer consoles and always let me download the games I wanted to play. Best of all, he had a big black Labrador called Bessie. We always kept it secret that instead of an after-school snack of carrot sticks we would have Nutella on toast most days.

Uncle Joe worked from home, so he was always in when I arrived. Uncle Joe knew how to fix almost anything. He fixed my laptop when I broke it, he fixed Mum's washing machine when it flooded all over the floor and he fixed my necklace with a pony on it that I got for Christmas. I should remember to tell him about my broken watch. He was a proper scientist that seemed to know how almost anything worked but he hadn't kept too well the last few years and liked to work from the house running a small repair business.

"Uncle Joe, can I do my homework here with you?" I'd ask him.

"Yeah Poppet, takes half the time for you when I'm telling you the answers I bet," he would say, laughing.

Uncle Joe had a great hug. Not the polite ones that you had to do with relatives you hardly saw that you were just desperate to be over. Great ones that let you know how much he adored you. His arms could reach all the way around me and if he stood up off the couch, he towered over me. Before he had become unwell he had loved running so keeping himself fit and active was natural to him.

He was Mum's favourite brother as well and he always said Mum was the brains of the family. "If she hadn't gone off to be an eco-warrior, she would have gone a lot further than recycling plants, but someone has to save the planet I suppose," he told me one day. "The thing about your mum, Lilly, is she is a grafter. She always has been. Never off sick. She would do any job rather than be sitting on her bum all day."

Uncle Joe was right. Mum did always work hard and long hours. I suppose she needed to as well as she was always telling me the mortgage and bills were massive.

"Hey, is that you, Lilly? You're late today, your Nutella's getting cold."

"Sorry, Uncle Joe, I decided to walk back across the fields today." I glanced up and saw his face free of facial hair and knew that meant he was having a good day.

"Did you stop to see the field of ponies? You were a while."

"Yeah, some of them came up to the fence and let me pet them. There's one with a long mane; it's lovely."

"Take some apples out of the fruit bowl and put them in your bag for tomorrow if you're walking that way. Bessie and I went down that way today and there's only three left now."

"Do you know why? There used to be loads. I noticed there were only three left as well."

"Not sure. If it's not science I don't know it. The field might be getting sold for building more houses or something; everywhere else is. Eat your snack up and we can try and get your homework done before your mum gets here. Unless you want to play the PlayStation with me instead?"

"If I get all my homework done tonight, can you take me over to the riding school on Wednesday night? Not to ride or anything, but just to watch? There's a show and my new friend is going to be in it. We will be back long before Mum."

"We'll see," said Uncle Joe.

It was our private joke that we had always had. *We'll see*, always meant yes with Uncle Joe. He was amazing.

"Who's your new friend?"

"She's fab, Uncle Joe; you'd like her. She invited me to go to a show with her at the weekend, but Mum says no."

"Why?"

"She doesn't know Kalila or her mum. Stranger Danger and all that. I'm desperate to go. I want to go more than anything. I'll even do all the dishes for a week."

"I can't drive you this weekend if that's what you're asking, because I have plans with my friends."

"I was going to get to go in the horse lorry and everything with them. Would you let me pretend I was here? Mum doesn't need to know."

"Yeah, your mum would kill me. She used to beat me up when I was the age you are now. I don't want to start her off doing that again," he joked.

I tried to forget the show and focused on the here and now. Decisions, decisions, I thought as I munched my snack, melting into the massive couch Uncle Joe had that made me feel safe and homely. I loved that couch. The issue with the decision was that Uncle Joe was great for helping get through homework fast but then he was great fun for playing computer games too.

"Can we do my maths now, and come up with some ideas for my science project while we play on the console?"

Uncle Joe went into the drawer and took out the pencils he kept for me doing my homework there and said, "Just don't destroy my village in the game this time" and he smiled.

"By the way," I said, "Andrew's mum was asking about you. Says you have to ring sometime."

Uncle Joe said, "She's a nice woman but she's not my type. She's been coming around a lot since I fixed her power washer. Don't know what I'm going to do if she needs any more repairs and I can't hide anymore." He was always funny and could make anything seem okay. He even used to tell me, "We have matching specs because these are the specs of cool people."

I didn't want to hurt Uncle Joe's feelings, so I didn't tell him our specs aren't cool.

Six

Chapter 6

"Lilly, get your school bag; you're going to be late."

"So, what do you fancy for your birthday then?" Mum asked.

"Hmmmm, I'm not sure." I'd love my own riding hat, but then I needed new boots too. I'd love one of the own a pony days at the stable but maybe that was too big a thing to ask for. Or a riding lesson?

"There must be something."

"I'd really like a pet, Mum; what about a hamster?"

I could dress my hamster up as a pony and make little outfits and little show jumps for it. I'd have a friend all the time.

"No pets, sweetheart, I can't take any more responsibility. Is there nothing else that you'd like? What about something to do with ponies?"

"Can I think about it more?"

"Oh yeah, but nothing with loads of packaging or bulky plastic that's going to go to the landfill."

Mum kissed me when she stopped the car. I wasn't quick enough to open the door handle and pop out before her lips connected with my cheek.

"Come on Mum, you get to drive away. I have to go and face all the kids that just saw you kiss me."

"Sorry, have a good day."

I hoped none of the kids from my class had seen me. Things were hard enough at school as it was. I went into the classroom and tried to take my usual seat, hoping Mrs Brown had forgotten she had moved me tables.

"Good morning."

"Good morning, Mrs Brown," we all sang back at her.

"Lilly, I moved your seat to the other table yesterday; that's your usual seat now."

So today wasn't the day that Mrs Brown was going to be forgetful then. She forgot about the spelling test on a Thursday once and we didn't get tested on the words. This was ideal as I had spent the evening before throwing sticks for Bessie in the garden with Uncle Joe instead of going over my words. I picked up my stuff and looked sadly at Rebecca as I moved away from her and over to my new seat between the two witches.

"Oh God, not you again," said Natasha as I sat down between her and Erin.

Andrew asked, "Lilly, why don't you tell Natasha to get lost?"

Natasha threw her pencil case at Andrew. "Because I'm the boss at this table. Now, shut up."

I looked down at my desk, wishing I was still sitting beside Rebecca or better still was able to speak up. I didn't understand why Natasha was so mean.

Mrs Brown said, " It's science week so I want to talk to you all about some of my favourite scientists and inventors. I hope you've all been working on your own inventions at home."

Seven

Chapter 7

Home-time came round, and I walked through the fields to avoid the drama of the school bus. When I got to the field of ponies, I saw an old man with a black and white dog throwing some hay in beside the ponies. I ran over and asked, "Hey, do you mind if I pat your ponies?"

His unwashed aroma still managed to surprise me with its fierceness, despite his stained old clothes giving me pre-warning. An old smelly man, with rips in his clothes, that looked as if he'd been rolling in the mud of the ponies' fields before he had started rolling in the hay.

He ignored me and carried on throwing the hay into the field from the back of his quad bike that he must have used to bring it down to the field.

"Can I pat your dog then?" I asked him.

The collie stood patiently by his quad bike looking like it might not have had a pat in a while.

I was surprised by how cranky his voice was when he answered, "No hen, it's not that kinda dog. It's a working dog and it might give you a bit of a nip. "

"Am I allowed to pet the ponies?" I tried again.

As he was done throwing the hay and ready to leave, he turned to look at me and said,

"Won't make any difference to me, pet them all you like. The black one is only here until the chestnut mare and foal are off to their new home, anyways, then it's time for a bullet for it."

I thought it was some type of grumpy old man joke that I didn't understand. Grumpy old men often have jokes that make no sense.

"Why don't you sell the black one too rather than shoot it then?" I panicked. I couldn't understand why someone would even think of shooting a healthy animal.

"Too much bother. All the adverts are on the internet now and I'm nae learning that just to sell a horse. Then all the people coming and going with their stupid questions. I bought it as part of a job lot of ponies at a sale. I don't even know if it's done anything and I've no way of finding out. Less hassle just to get it away."

"Can I help? I can put an advert up online and show people the horse if you like?" I pleaded.

"I need it gone in the next few days. No time. There's no point getting all sentimental over animals, plenty more ponies out there" he had gone from growling to barking. I couldn't figure out if his annoyance was at the particular questions I was asking him or having to communicate when he didn't enjoy that sort of thing. I had to keep on though as a pony's life was at stake here.

I asked him, "Can I have it then? I would love a pony."

"Aye lass, save me the cost of a bullet, no money in horses anymore. Don't know what made me try selling them instead of cows. Once the mare and foal are away, I don't need an extra animal to throw hay into."

"Really, a pony, I can take a pony? I'll ask Uncle Joe; he is amazing with animals."

"I don't think some daft kid has a place to take a pony, now on you go." And he climbed onto his quad bike and drove off up into the distance.

I ran the rest of the way home.

"Uncle Joe, Uncle Joe, the farmer...ponies...said I could have it...bullet..."

A jumble of words came out in no particular order. Uncle Joe put his games controller on the couch and stood up. Bessie bounded up to meet me.

"Lilly, what's wrong?"

"The farmer with the ponies. There are only three left and he has the mare and foal to go and he can't sell the last one. He plans to shoot it and he says that I can have it instead. I need the pony, Uncle Joe. It can live in your garden, and I can look after it and brush it and ride it."

Uncle Joe smiled and said, "Lilly, there are times that you are so grown up and other times you are still just a kid. What do I think my neighbours would say if I put a pony in the garden? How would we look after it? Do you think if it's a nice, sweet, healthy pony with no problems the farmer is going to shoot it? Farmers have livestock for the money. He will sell it and if he can't...well that's his business. It will be old or sick or something."

I was trying not to cry now
. "Uncle Joe, he really said he will shoot it. I swear he said that. He just needs it gone quickly because he sold the land."

Uncle Joe said, "The crabbit old farmer from down the road is always talking about shooting something. He threatens to shoot the dogs that get in his field in case they bother the sheep. He probably doesn't have his kids at home anymore because he threatened to shoot them too. Honestly, he is just a haverer. Don't you worry.

Anyway, your Nutella and toast is ready." Uncle Joe always said yes, especially with really important things, but this time was different. I felt a ball of sadness in my belly. I couldn't understand why Uncle Joe wouldn't listen. He always understood when things were important to me, and this was the most important thing ever, and he'd dismissed it right away." Uncle Joe hugged me and said, "You're so upset, let's not talk about it anymore, but it's not realistic for you to have a pony with the cost of feeding and hiring a stable. And anyway, if I were able to make it so you could have a pony, I would make sure you got the very best one."

I sadly melted into the couch and Bessie climbed up and snuggled in beside me. "I wish people were all as straightforward as you, Bessie."

Most of the good telly had finished by the time I had calmed down from chatting with the farmer. Uncle Joe had turned the computer off when he saw how upset I was and let me watch all the kids' shows on TV. Uncle Joe even got some chocolate out and said, "Come on Lilly, have a wee sweetie, my wee sweetie." That was Uncle Joe's favourite joke; he used it every time he offered me some sweets. Scottish people often said wee for small and not for a pee. It confused the new girl at the yard when she moved in with her own pony because she lived in England before, so she thought wee was like when the horse peed.

"How about a nice walk with Bessie? I will let you throw the stick."

I shook my head.

Uncle Joe looked thoughtful. "Hm, I wouldn't mind a word with that old farmer for upsetting you like that. What would you like to do, then?"

I thought for a minute and looked at the clock. We still had some time with Mum working late. "Can we work on my science project?

You're like a proper inventor so you'd be amazing at helping me invent things and I have an idea of what I want to make."

Uncle Joe said, "Come on then, I have a fab workshop of goodies out there to make stuff from," and he turned and walked out to the workshop with Bessie at his feet.

I always liked going into the workshop. I loved that Uncle Joe trusted me now in his workshop. Uncle Joe used to worry when I was little that I could fall over and break things that he was working on. Sometimes he would work on his inventions and other times he would work on repairing things like vacuum cleaners and other small electrical things.

"Uncle Joe, what made you want to be a scientist?"

"If I hadn't been a scientist and didn't work from my workshop, I wouldn't get to hang out with you and Bessie every afternoon."

I looked over at Joe and smiled. Uncle Joe knew what I meant just as well with a smile as if I had used a thousand words.

"Mum says you used to work in a big science laboratory with a white coat and everything. Do you miss it?"

"Not when I get to see you every day, and this way when my health is good, I can work away and when it's not so good I can chill with Bessie. I can't always tell how I am going to be from one day to the next, so I like being able to just work for myself from home— and of course, hang out with you and get plenty of time with my friends."

There were always all sorts of crazy goodies in the workshop and not just the sweets and juice type of goodies he kept in the drawer of his big old desk. Uncle Joe always had a project he was working on, whether it was fixing something for someone or whether it was inventing something new.

I walked around the workshop picking all the things up and asking what they were for. "What's this for?"

"Oh, it's an old fence energiser. It's expensive to buy a new one so I'm going to try and fix this one up with my soldering iron later. You can help if you like."

I spied a machine with a white dust sheet over the top.

"What's under there?"

Bessie was lying under one of the desks and chewing a stick to death. Poor stick.

Uncle Joe said, "Oh that's just a wee invention for me that I'm working on for myself. Imagine if I could make myself extraordinarily small and travel the world that way."

"That's cool. Does it work yet?"

"Nah, of course not, it's quite far-fetched. It's to shrink things down. That way I could get all over the world, like the big science fair in China I wanted to go to—just post myself with no airfare, plenty of juice and snacks and I would be fine—all in micro mini size of course. I could go economy small parcel."

I tugged off the white dust sheet and looked at it.

"That's amazing, Uncle Joe. How do you get it to work?"

Uncle Joe said, "Well I can use it for other things too, like posting food to countries where people don't have enough. If it was ever to work of course—it's called a minimising microscope. It uses implosion fabrication, and it can reduce anything to nanoscale. Well, it would, but we have hit a few snags."

I peered at the machine. It was amazing to think it could do something so awesome as to reduce the size of anything—even a person. If of course, it was ever to work. It was placed in an old box about half the size of a shoebox that Uncle Joe must have made from wood. "What does it need to work?"

"That's the question. Bessie and I are a bit stuck. We need to find the strength of the lens to fit in it. And, with it being nanoscale we need to find the right power source. I started trying to shrink down my favourite mug." Uncle Joe pulled out a mug I had bought him on holiday last year which said, "Inventors keep on trying."

"Watch. I'll show you how far I got, which isn't far, so don't get your hopes up."

Uncle Joe put the mug down with the lens aiming at it as he continued to explain.

"The thing is, the machine just fries as the power sources are all too strong. They need to be nanoscale too. I went from plugging it in at the wall to an old car battery, and then some small double AA batteries from the shop. I would need to make a really small power cell, I think. This is the fourth prototype, as I keep frying them all."

I couldn't hide the fact that I was impressed.

"That's amazing, Uncle Joe. Can we work on that for my school science project?"

"Remember ethics honey, you need to enter something that is your own work. I can help you with bits but the idea and the knowledge have to come from you - even if I teach you the knowledge you need to do the project" Uncle Joe said

"Well how about we do this not for the school fair but just for fun?"

Uncle Joe smiled at my enthusiasm.

"I don't think we will get this working any time soon. I am sure this will be a longer-term project. Sometimes stuff just doesn't ever quite get there at all and I think this may be one of those things. In fact, if you can fix it, you can keep it. Pretty sure that this will still be sitting there in its box when you're finished school and university and it will still be waiting on being fixed. "

"If I can fix it I can keep it?....really?" The possibilities filled my head with the ideas jumping from one to the next.

"The chances are you will be grown up and married with your own children before the technology to make this work exists, but I love that you are willing to try. That's how the best inventors work. Try when nobody else believes it can happen"

I watched Uncle Joe as he put the sheet back over the machine.

"I won't get married, and have lots of children, Uncle Joe. When I'm fully grown, I'm going to have lots of ponies instead and become a famous showjumper."

"Sounds reasonable." Uncle Joe smiled. "Right, let's get started on this school project of making something before your mum gets back. My friend Dave is coming over tonight for a few beers when Mum collects you so I will need some time to clean up a bit first."

I didn't understand why adults cleaned up for other adults coming over. Surely if they were all doing it for each other, they could just leave it as it was, and it wouldn't matter. They could just admit to each other how messy they all were and agree not to tidy for each other's visits.

"Well, I wanted to make a full working clock. I saw in a book how you could make them, and we could put it on a wooden background, and I could paint a unicorn on it," I said enthusiastically.

"Okay, that could work," Uncle Joe said.

My many ideas all started bursting out of my head now that I knew we were in the cave of possibilities that was Uncle Joe's workshop.

"Or even better, we could make a wee obstacle course with show jumps for hamsters. Mum might get me a hamster for my birthday and then I can dress it as a pony and make it go through the course." Of course, I wanted the actual pony but if I focused on the hamster, Mum was more likely to cave in. Especially when she saw my amazing invention.

"Okay, so what do we need to make this? Do you have a drawing of your design?"

I pulled out a picture I had drawn and hidden it in the back of my maths jotter. I had done it earlier when I had finished my sums and was waiting for the rest of my group to finish. I was in the yellow group which meant it was supposed to be ultra-hard, but as Uncle Joe had shown me how to do loads of maths, I was quite fast at it.

"Okay, here's some scraps of leftover wood to make the box to put the course in. If we build the box first, we can put your course of jumps in after. Now, I have wee nails and bits of wood to make the show jumps out of if you look in that box under the desk over there." Uncle Joe pointed to a big box filled with wooden offcuts. At least, we wouldn't be short of material.

Uncle Joe put a tin for storing nails on the table and placed a hammer alongside it. I loved how Uncle Joe had loads and loads of jars and tins, all filled with nails and screws in all different colours, sizes, and widths. There was no end of options of what to use when we started to make stuff.

There's a technique for most tools, and as long as I used them properly as I had been shown, I was allowed to use anything. I thought about how much better my wooden invention would be this year than last year's. Uncle Joe had been unwell, so I had made it with Mum and had binoculars from cling film and toilet roll tubes. It all got soaked in the rain on the way to school as if it hadn't been rubbish enough to start with. Natasha laughed and said that her little sister at nursery could have made a better science project.

I pulled out my special safety goggles and gloves that Uncle Joe kept beside his own safety goggles for when we were working on our joint projects.

Uncle Joe helped me to work out the size of the wood to use, and we measured and started to cut it to the right size.

"Can I use the saw this time myself?" I asked him.

"Sure. Do you want to mark the pencil line on the wood first so we can see where to cut?"

"Yeah," I said as I pulled the tape measure along the wood to mark the right length.

Just as I was about to draw the pencil line on the wood, I heard the crunching of some feet coming up the drive to the workshop. Uncle Joe went to see who it was. It must have been someone he knew as I heard Uncle Joe begin speaking to them.

"Hey there, I managed to get your lawnmower going earlier. It was just a blocked carburettor. If you reverse your van up the drive it will be easier to lift it in."

"That's fab," said a woman's voice. "I didn't want to fork out for a new one, and as your sister would say, it's just another thing for landfill if we go straight to buying a new one."

"Yeah, it's always best to repair—save yourself some money as well. She loves working at the recycling plant; she has some great ideas for new ways to help the environment. She talks about all the changes she wants to make there."

"I've not seen her in ages. How're things with you?"

The grown-ups started to drone on about loads of adult stuff. They chatted away about all the boring stuff of who was up to what, like who had a new job or was moving house. I tried to wait for Uncle Joe but knowing that this boring adult chat could go on for some time I carried on until I was done cutting up all the wood. I waited. And waited. I listened at the door.

"Yeah, Bessie did that with an old pair of socks one time, and..." I knew now the conversation had turned to dogs; they would be there a while.

I moved over and sat on the stool by Uncle Joe's new machine for making things smaller. I took the white sheet back off for a better look. Maybe I could impress Uncle Joe and fix it for him. I thought about trying to nail the bits of wood for my project together while I waited, but I knew I wasn't allowed to use the hammer or drill when he was away. I waited more. I thought about the problem with the power source on the minimising microscope.

I still had my unicorn watch that had stopped working last month. I kept wearing it because I liked the unicorns and I thought if I had it with me, I might remember to ask Uncle Joe to help me fix it one day when we weren't playing computer games.

I heard the woman laughing with Uncle Joe from outside the workshop. Did you ever notice that adults tell the same jokes over and over...like Mum had the one about, "Don't spend it all at once," when she gave me 50p for a pint of milk at the shop when she knew it cost 50p for a pint of milk at the shop. She made the joke every time even though we didn't laugh at it anymore, in fact, we didn't laugh at it the first time. But most weeks I would be sent for milk, and she would give me 50p and tell me not to spend it all at once.

I decided to try and fix my broken watch myself while I was waiting so I took it off to get a proper look. There were small holes in the back that needed a screwdriver to undo them. I popped off my seat and fetched the wee screwdrivers to try and take off the small screws in the holes. It was tricky at first as the holes were so tiny, but with my specs, my eyesight is pretty perfect, so I could get right to the screws.

Once the screws were off, I picked my watch up, and out of the back fell a silver coin-shaped battery. I thought my watch was probably low on battery like the time that the remote for the television ran out. I didn't think I'd seen a battery like this before, so I was stuck until Uncle Joe came back. I could ask him if he had a new battery of the same unusual shape and size.

It was so small that I worried it might get lost. I didn't want it to fall on the floor and get kicked into a drain or something before

I showed him, or how would he know what size it was. I wandered over and clipped it into the crocodile clips that Joe had used to attach the last battery he tried on his minimising microscope. My attention returned to hoping I could try and fix the minimising telescope while I was waiting. How awesome would it be if I could fix something for Uncle Joe for a change? I took a swig of my juice and put it down on the table and had a look. The science part of my brain kicked in and I remembered he said he needed a lens, and he didn't have the right one. Hmmm... What else has lenses? I wondered. Cameras have lenses. When I went to Rebecca's, her big brother had a fancy one. He used to take pictures of her puppies and he had all different lenses he could put on his camera.

The only lens I had was on my face, my glasses. I took the lens that was already in the machine out and replaced it by popping my glasses on it. I put my glass of juice in its site and pressed the button absentmindedly. I didn't expect anything. If an amazing scientist like Uncle Joe couldn't fix it, what chance did I have?

"Whirr-whirr-whirr" The machine made noises. I was so excited. Bessie must have heard the noises as she ran into the shed to see what was happening. Bessie jumped up to have a look and knocked over the juice.

"Oh, Bessie, what a mess!" I patted her head. I hated getting a row for spilling drinks and I'm sure Bessie would have felt the same way. I was about to get some of the old rags kept in the corner to wipe up the juice when I heard a new noise and stopped to see where it was coming from. The machine whirred and buzzed, and a laser of light came, lighting up Bessie. Bessie barked excitedly then, *poomphhh*.

Suddenly Bessie was tiny, like *really* tiny.

"Oh Bessie, you're smaller than a pet mouse. The machine works!" I couldn't believe what I was seeing. "Bessie, is this real? It's like being in a cartoon!"

"*Woof! Woof!*"

The quietest barking noises came from Bessie as she ran up and down the table. She picked up one of the screws and put it down in front of me like a stick for me to throw for her. I scooped her up gently and put her in one of the empty tins Uncle Joe had lying around so she didn't get lost or hurt.

"We best get Uncle Joe. It's amazing that the minimising microscope works but I don't know what he will say about you being smaller than a mouse."

"*Woof-woof!*" barked Bessie.

"Maybe the postman will like this version of you better though," I told Bessie.

Uncle Joe put his head around the door. "Lilly, Janet came round to pick up a lawnmower I was fixing for her and now her car isn't starting. I'm going to have a look at it. Your mum will be here soon. I'll be out on the driveway if you need me."

"Uncle Joe, Bessie came in and—"

"Yeah. That's okay, you keep her here for the company. I'll be right back. Bye."

He closed the door over, and I heard his feet crunch back up to the top of the driveway.

"Oh, what have I done? Oh, Bessie, I am so sorry, you're going to be the world's smallest Labrador. I don't know how to sort you." I remembered what Uncle Joe always told me. "Don't worry about messing around with broken things. If it's already broken, then it can't get any more broken. Sometimes it's the fiddling that sorts it."

As his voice rang in my head, I tried to be calm, so Bessie wasn't scared.

"Bessie, stay still, we need to sort this. I know just what to do." I didn't, though Bessie worked out quickly how to leap out of the tin despite it being well above her chest height with her shrunk downsize.

"Oh yeah, I forgot you're a labrador, you can escape anything as a party trick," I told her. Bessie ran up and down, so I made her a little playpen out of bits of wood lying around from the hamster project, this time three times the height of Bessie with a little mesh over the top I found to keep her in. With her safely out of the way, I could tinker around with the machine.

I had flipped the lens around so the bottom was now the top. Would it do the opposite and turn into a maximising telescope and make Bessie big again? I hoped she wouldn't be too big, or I might end up with a horse-sized Bessie.

"Okay, I'm ready now, stay still. Here we go." I aimed the laser in Bessie's direction and pressed the button, hoping it would work.

Whirr-whirr-whirr bang. The laser came out a second time. I was so surprised and before I knew it, a full-sized Bessie was standing on the table. One paw was in the wooden box that I had made for her, and the mesh lay on the top to keep her on was at the top of her head. She jumped down, knocking over all the bits of wood.

I petted her. "Wow, Bessie, you're normal size again. I was scared when I wasn't sure how to make you big again. My word, Bessie, don't we have an amazing secret. Now, don't tell a soul."

"Woof-woof," said Bessie, back at her normal volume.

I heard a crunching sound on the gravel outside again telling me someone was coming up the drive.

"Lilly, are you in the workshop?" came Mum's voice.

I knew exactly what to do.

"Yeah Mum, I'm in here with Bessie. Uncle Joe is just trying to sort Janet's car. I think it broke down when she came to collect something he repaired for her."

Mum opened the door to the workshop and said,

"Hey, Lilly." She opened her arms for a hug. "Are you ready? I missed you today."

"Yeah, Mum, just let me grab my science project that I've been working on for school."

I popped my glasses back on my face. I left the hamster show-jumping kit we were working on and threw the white sheet over it in the corner where the minimising microscope had been. I remembered Uncle Joe had said, "If you can fix it, you can keep it"—even if it was just because he didn't think there would be any fixing it.

I put the minimising microscope in my backpack. I knew exactly what had to be done with it.

Eight

Chapter 8

All the next day at school I was waiting for the day to be over. Nothing could bother me. I wasn't going to get upset that I couldn't get to sit beside Rebecca. I wasn't going to get upset that I had to sit beside Natasha and Erin. I didn't even care that all Erin and Natasha were talking about was the fun that they were going to have at the riding school in the show on Wednesday or that smart mouth Natasha had thought of a new name of *Silly Lilly Bogey Head* for me. When the school bell rang at the end of the day, I didn't lurk around hiding till everyone had left.

"Gotta run, Rebecca, I'll speak to you tomorrow," I told her as I dashed off out of the classroom and through the school gates.

"How come you never run that fast in gym class?" Rebecca called out after me.

I would have told her about it, but nobody could know my special secret. I ran through the paths at the back of the school, as fast as my legs would get me. I saw the mare and foal had gone, leaving just the beautiful black pony in the field.

"Hey gorgeous, are your friends away to their new home? Don't be scared. I have a plan, so the nasty farmer won't get a chance to shoot you. Would you like to come home with me?"

The pony let me stroke her face gently. I took that as a *Yes*.

"I don't have room for a normal-sized pony, so I'm going to have to make a special arrangement for you, okay? But it will keep you safe if it works."

She must have understood because she stood patiently as I put my bag over the fence and climbed over beside it. I stood beside the pony and gave her face and neck a good stroke and she came closer to me, enjoying the attention. I pulled out my lunchbox from that morning and stabbed holes in the lid with the scissors I had borrowed from the art corner. I set the minimising microscope up and took off my glasses to place them where the lens should be.

"Oh, I so hope this works again. What if I have the lens the wrong way?"

I took her not running away as an agreement. I aimed the laser at her and pressed the button. Nothing happened.

"Oh crap," I said as I saw the farmer on the other side of the field with his quad bike.

He had his back turned to me as he was fixing some fencing, but I knew he could be over on his quad bike quicker than I could run away with a pony—a pony that I couldn't lift over the fence or get out through the gate that had a big padlock on it. I know that he had said he was going to shoot it, but he might have felt differently at me interfering once I tried taking the pony away.

The pony nudged my hand as I was fiddling with the machine, trying to work out where I had gone wrong.

"Oh yeah, the on/off switch. I need to turn that on before I press the button. Let's see what happens this time, pony." I flicked the switch and pressed the button.

Whirrrr-whirrr! Bang-bang! A light came out and I was too scared to look. I closed my eyes and pressed them shut.

"Please be small, please be small," I hoped aloud.

I opened my eyes, and the pony was no longer standing over me. I looked down and saw the teeniest tiniest pony, no bigger than a hamster. I looked up at the field to see the farmer turn around to catch sight of me at that very moment.

"What are you doing in my field?" the farmer bellowed. I realised that he could see me but at that distance, he couldn't see a hamster sized pony. He jumped on his quad bike and started to ride over, shouting.

"Quick!" I told the pony.

I bent down, scooped it up, put it in my lunchbox and pressed the lid on. I hurriedly put the minimising microscope back in my bag and threw it on my back. With the lunchbox still in my hand, I scrambled over the fence and ran as fast as my legs would go towards Uncle Joe's. When I was too out of puff to keep going, I stopped and went into some of the thick trees and forestry to catch my breath where the farmer wouldn't be able to see me. I peeked in the box.

"Don't be scared, tiny pony. I had to get you away from the farmer. I'll look after you so well. I've always wanted a pony so, so much."

The tiny pony looked back at me.

"Are you hungry?" I asked her.

I picked some grass from the ground and put it in the lunch box and the sweet pony started to munch on it straight away.

"That's it, tiny pony, you enjoy your snack. Do you want to be my tiny pony now? I promise to look after you. Tiny would be a lovely name for you."

Tiny looked up and I knew she was mine.

It was hard to tell what colour Tiny was exactly. Tiny was so muddy she looked a very dark brown or black under all that matted hair with clumps of mud on her. I didn't need to know what her coat was like to know that I loved her already. I walked calmly the rest of the way to Uncle Joe's and stopped the last little bit of the way to put my lunch box in my backpack.

"Don't be scared Tiny, I just need to hide you for now."

I opened the front door to Uncle Joe's and shouted out,

"Hey, it's just me."

It was a strange little ritual we did every day because it was always just me at that time of day.

Uncle Joe was sitting on the couch and looked up.

"Hey, my Lilly, it's Nutella and toast time. You are looking very pleased with yourself today."

"Am I?" I tried to look innocent.

"Yeah, it's nice to see you looking so happy. What happened? Good day at school?"

"Great day."

"Okay, well I'm making our snack. Are we gaming first this evening first?" he asked.

I wanted to lock myself in the bathroom and play with my pony in private all night, but I couldn't really explain that to Uncle Joe.

"Erm, well I have some science homework to do, all about science ethics and stuff and then can we work on my hamster course maybe?" I could keep Tiny in it until I figured something else out, I thought.

"Okay. That's a great idea. We can get stuck into the homework, and then we will have plenty of time to go to your thing at the riding school tomorrow. What do we need to do for science homework?" asked Uncle Joe.

Uncle Joe always made me feel that he wanted to spend time with me, and it made our afternoons cool.

"We're studying all inventors and we have to write down three examples of when someone invented something really good and later regretted it."

"Right, I'll make tea to go with the toast and you get googling on the computer."

I typed in *Inventors with regrets* to the search engine. I wanted to get finished quickly so I could sneak off and check Tiny. I skimmed down the page of search results and picked out some of the most interesting things I could see.

"I've got some ideas from the internet search. There's this guy who invented the guillotine and then they used it to kill him, according to this website."

"Really?" said Uncle Joe. "I didn't know about that. I was thinking more of the guy who learnt to split the atom and got a Nobel Prize for it."

"Nobel Prize. Wasn't he really happy?"

"Not when they used the discovery to start making nuclear bombs that could kill loads of people and destroy whole countries. Bet the inventor was having a bad day when he woke up that morning." Uncle Joe popped my cup of tea in front of me to go with my toast.

"Yeah, that would be a bit of a bad day."

I panicked on the inside realising that brilliant inventions could be used for bad things. I realised that it was important nobody else found out that the minimising microscope was working. A big secret. If nobody knew about the invention, then nobody could ever use it for anything bad. I wasn't planning on telling anyone as it was, but this made keeping the secret a far bigger responsibility than I had first realised. Bessie watched me bite into my toast, hoping I would give her some. I was desperate to get off on my own so I could check on Tiny. I jumped up and grabbed my school bag and headed to the toilet. I gently took my packed lunch box out and peered in.

"Neigh! Neigh!" called out Tiny.

"What am I going to do with you, Tiny? I can't keep you in there forever. Come on out and stretch your legs and I'll get you a drink."

I scooped Tiny up and put her in the bath, and she went for a canter around. The bath was slippery for her pony hooves, and she skidded and fell. Her mini pony body fell and she slid along the bath on her tummy.

"Tiny! Oh no!"

I scooped her up, terrified she had injured herself. "I saw a man on horse racing on TV say if horses break their legs they need to be put to sleep, please don't fall over in the bath." I looked around for somewhere safe to put Tiny. If I put her on the toilet seat it was quite a drop-down for a pony that could fit in my hand if she was to fall. Maybe the safest place was the floor. I put her down gently and told her, "Okay, Tiny, I'll get you some water. Now what to put it in?" I looked around and the only thing I could see was the soap dish by the sink. Hmm, too many gunky bits of soap in there to make the water taste all funny. I looked in the cupboard under the sink and saw a small clear plastic container that Uncle Joe used to keep his toiletries organised. I pulled it out and popped the cans of deodorant, shaving foam, aftershave, and shower gels back into the cupboard keeping the container on the floor. I washed out all the gunky bits of soap and dust stuck around the rim and filled it up with fresh clear water. I took a sip to make sure it didn't taste weird. Perfect.

"Here you go, Tiny. It's nice and safe on the ground." I placed it down. Tiny came running over to see what the container was and gave it a sniff. She climbed up putting her front legs up over the container and had a look inside. She pushed her nose into the water and shook her head in surprise that the water was wet. My throat tickled as I tried to hold back my laughter and coughed to cover up the laughing sounds. Tiny spooked at my coughing and panicked, jumping into the dish. Oh, my goodness, a wet mini pony swimming around in the container. Tiny seemed to be great in the water and was circling like a strong swimmer, but I quickly scooped her out.

"Be careful, Tiny, now how am I going to dry you off? I can't ask Uncle Joe for the hairdryer without him getting suspicious. If he even has a hairdryer. I haven't ever seen one here anyway" I thought aloud and shared my thoughts with my new special friend as though she may help me come up with an answer.

Tiny stood in my hand and shook hard like a wet dog. The droplets flew off Tiny's coat and splattered my face and I smiled so widely that some of the water landed on my tongue.

"You okay there, pet? I saw you take your bag in with you, do you need any help?" Uncle Joe called.

"No, I'll be right out Uncle Joe, I'm just fine." I picked up the hand towel and dried it to get off as much of the wet as possible that was left since Tiny's big dog shake. I didn't want her getting a cold and mum always told me I might get a cold if I didn't dry my hair properly before I went out. I lowered my voice to a whisper. "Okay Tiny, I'll put you in my pocket just now while we go out and do my homework so I can know that you're okay. Don't move around too much." I popped Tiny into my skirt pocket; skirts with pockets are such a splendid idea.

"Right Uncle Joe, I'm ready to finish my homework. Where were we?"

"You have the guy who invented the guillotine, and the guy who split the atom and had it turned into bombs. You need to write down one more."

I felt Tiny wriggling in my pocket and put my hand in to reassure her. I put my other hand on the mouse of Uncle Joe's computer and scrolled down for more results that might give inspiration for the science homework until something caught my eye. It wasn't easy with one hand on the mouse, one on Tiny and trying to read at the same time. Maybe it would be better if I could think of something, so I didn't have to try and use the computer too much right now. "What about the guy who invented gunpowder? That was initially meant to help people. It was medicinal and then used to kill people. We did that in class."

"That's a good one; I didn't know that one."

Bessie jumped up at me, barking and sniffing my pocket. I pushed her down. "No, Bessie."

I could tell she was scaring Tiny as the more Bessie barked, the more Tiny kicked and wriggled.

Uncle Joe's voice turned low and strict as he said,

"Bessie, get down. What's wrong with you? *Bed. Now!*"

Bessie put her head low and slunk off to her bed.

"Oh, you never shout at anyone. Poor Bessie, she didn't mean any harm." I hadn't seen Bessie getting into trouble before and felt guilty. It would not have happened if I hadn't been sneaking a super small pony around in my pocket.

"She was acting strangely and no matter how much you love an animal it has to know its place. I can't have Bessie jumping all over you and scratching you and getting away with it."

I turned and started to walk towards Bessie's bed, but Uncle Joe stopped me.

"I know it's hard, Lilly, but don't go and pet the dog just now. Bessie has to learn."

Now Bessie was in trouble, and it was all my fault, and Tiny was nervously squirming in my pocket.

"Come on, let's get out and work on your science project for school and then I can take you to that horsey thing tomorrow night, and we can talk about what you want for your birthday this year. Any ideas?"

"One sec, Uncle Joe, I'll just nip to the loo first."

"Okay. If there's anything you want help with or need to talk about just let me know. I know I'm a guy, but if you need me to go and get anything or whatever..."

My cheeks burned, but it was better Uncle Joe suspected I kept running to the bathroom with my bag because I had started my periods for the first time than knowing I had a secret little pony hiding in my pocket.

It took me a minute or two to put Tiny back in my packed lunch box with the breathing holes, place the box gently at the top of the school bag and take it out to the garage with me. In the workshop, there was a nice place to put my bag so I could leave it open and let the daylight in. I must try and pick some more grass on the way home.

Nine

Chapter 9

"Right, get your tool kit out. Guess what you will need first?" said Uncle Joe

"My tape measure."

"That's right. We always start with our tape measure and spirit level when we are making stuff. Now, what's the golden rule when we're building stuff?"

"Don't buy pink tools as they are always blunt and cheaply made. Buy normal tools and make them pink yourself if you need your tools to be pink!"

"Not that rule, though the pink tool rule is important. This rule is for when you are making things and already have the tools?"

"It has to be straight and level so it's strong. Use a spirit level where I can."

It was always great working with Uncle Joe. He let me use a proper saw instead of a kids' one that couldn't cut anything. He let me do stuff for myself when he had shown me once. The feeling of looking at something that I had built myself made me feel I had achieved something.

Uncle Joe and I built away working on a little hamster show jumping course in a lovely little box.

"I think when your mum sees this, she's bound to let you get a hamster. Also, she will kill me for encouraging you."

I grinned and avoided the subject. "Why are pink tools always made so rubbish?"

"I think the people that manufacture them haven't met the same kind of girls I have, and it's usually girls who go for pink. Not always though. If I'm taking you to watch the show tomorrow, do you want me to book you some riding lessons for your birthday? You're not giving much away, so I'm gonna take a guess on what to get you."

My heart fluttered. "Yes, Uncle Joe, that would be amazing. I love the lessons that aren't helpers' lessons; they are much longer, and I want to learn."

After lots of banging and nailing and drilling and me focusing as hard as I could we had a hamster cage and hamster show-jumping course.

"It's amazing, Uncle Joe. I love it."

"Well, it's pretty strongly built, you did a great job with your joins. You are going to be a great fixer of broken things and inventor."

I looked over at my school bag with Tiny in it and thought *if only you knew.*

"Hey Joe, hey Lilly, you look as if you're both having fun." Mum had arrived.

"Hey Mum, yeah I was making things with Uncle Joe, all my homework's done as well."

"Lilly's a superhero, just like her mum." Uncle Joe told my mum with a smile. He was always nice to Mum.

Mum walked over to inspect my invention. "Oh, and it's all made from repurposed stuff, I see. I am impressed."

Typical Mum, to be more impressed by my recycling than the awesome building that we did.

"It's for school. We need to bring it home so I can take it to school as my project."

"Okay, well pop it in the boot, and I'll grab your bag," Mum said as she reached down and snatched up my school bag.

"Noooooooo! Be gentle."

"What's wrong with you? It's just your school bag!"

"I know, it's fine. I just mean, let me carry my bag, Mum," I said, taking it from her hand and gently zipping it up. Poor Tiny. It would be dark inside my bag now. I put it gently on my back and started carrying out my school stuff. Uncle Joe took one side of the hamster course and Mum took the other. They walked to mum's car boot and placed it gently inside whilst I took my bag on my back and carried the little cage. I kept a hold of the bag so it could come in the front with me knowing it had a special secret inside and popped the cage in the boot beside the hamster course.

"You know, she's so independent these days. I think that it's the one decent thing from the riding school visits," Mum said to Uncle Joe as though I wasn't there.

"Yeah, she's always been pretty capable. She can manage in here and she didn't get that much of a hand with her project. Lilly's quite grown up these days."

Oh God, Uncle Joe, don't mention my bathroom visits, I thought.

"Yeah, she does fend for herself. Especially lately as I've got a big thing on at work at the moment."

"Is this your plan to have less go to landfills at the plant project?"

"Yeah, I mean, if we could just recycle a few extra pieces of material, it would save so much extra going to landfill. It all adds up. It's getting the management to agree with me when recycling some of the stuff we don't do isn't that cost-effective, but I'm hunting for cheaper ways, and I might be onto something with rubber tyres."

"You always do well at problem-solving. Keep at what's important to you. I'm feeling great just now, so I was going to make the most of it and fancied taking Lilly over to this riding school thing tomorrow."

"Would you, Joe? That would be ace. I'm feeling so guilty for working all the time and I know Lilly will love it, even if she does stink when she comes home from the yard, and I'm a woman who specialises in rubbish!"

I waited. It's particularly annoying when adults get chatting and go on and on and expect you to wait. I was desperate to get off home and have some Tiny time. Finally, Mum turned to the car and said, "Right, do you have all your stuff?"

I had my stuff in the boot, except of course my precious bag with Tiny in it which I held on my lap all the way home.

I rushed to my bedroom as soon as I got home. There wasn't a lot of floor space left over with all my mess lying on the floor, so I kicked what I could of it under the bed, so Mum didn't see it when she gave me a hand carrying in the hamster jumping course. I knew if I didn't get the last few smelly socks hidden away then I would be told to tidy my room, and then she would check. That would include my kicking stuff under the bed trick so better to do it now. I ran downstairs banging every step with my feet clattering on every tread. "Mum, if I get the hamster cage myself can you help me with the hamster course out the boot," I asked her. Mum was in the bathroom "Can I not even have a pee in peace, Lilly. I never actually agreed I would get you a hamster you know, and if you bring it in out the car boot, we will just need to put it back in again to take it to school. It makes more sense just to leave it there for now"

"Please Mum, I don't need it at school for a few days yet and I want to decorate it nicely. Pleaaaaaassseeee" I knew she was tired and likely to cave in just for the peace if I kept pestering her and I needed it to put my special tiny pony in tonight. She helped me lug the course in and put it down on my newly cleared bedroom floor and I ran back and grabbed the hamster cage myself. I found a good spot and moved the hamster cage and jumping course into place.

"Hey Tiny," I said, bringing Tiny out of my bag. She was so sweet. I popped her into her cage and let her know, "You will be safe in there, sweetheart."

Tiny ran around the outside of her cage checking everything out with her little head thrown in the air. It made sense to me though, as I had read in my pony care book that horses always checked the perimeters of a new fence line when they were somewhere like a field they hadn't been in before for the first time. Tiny's mane flowed as she ran, and despite being no bigger than a hamster she was so majestic. Just in miniature. She was still muddy, though, with huge clumps of mud all over her mane, tail, and body. I took the minimising microscope out and shoved it under the bed safely out of sight before I returned to watching little Tiny running around her new home.

"I'll look after you, and never let anything happen to you, I promise Tiny. I'll get you some nice bedding stuff and something to eat and drink."

The horses at the stables all had straw for their beds but I didn't have any of that. I didn't need much for Tiny, just a handful. I could phone Rebecca and ask her cos she had a hamster, and she had all that lying around anyway. If I was allowed a phone and a Facebook profile like the other kids in my class, I could ask her to bring it into school tomorrow. Oh...so annoying. I thought about going around to Rebecca's but it was too late now, and I wouldn't be allowed, plus I didn't want to leave my sweet Tiny.

"I know what to do, Tiny, I've still got loads of kids' toys, from when I was small. I can maybe make something from them for you."

I peeked into my huge doll's house that I wasn't allowed to throw out even though it was far too babyish now. I chucked the dolls from the house aside and pulled out the bed and popped it into my cage. Tiny ran over and jumped up onto the bed.

"There you go, Tiny, you've got a bed now," I told her.

I went back to the doll's house and spied the bath.

"Hmmm, maybe not too much water again, Tiny."

I wondered what would make a good water bucket for a hamster sized pony. I went downstairs and Mum was scrolling through her phone. I looked in the kitchen and hoped for some inspiration. Then I saw the ketchup bottle. I took the lid off and bolted back to Tiny in my room.

"Why are you rushing about like that Lilly, is everything okay?" Mum called.

"Yeah, all good, Mum," I called back, knowing she would go straight back to scrolling on her phone.

I imagined ponies didn't like ketchup too much, so it took me a while to rinse it all out and fill it with water. I popped it in the cage and Tiny ran over to investigate.

"Yeah, no swimming this time, not till I give you a proper bath, but a safe amount of water to drink from for when I'm not here. What do you make of that?"

Tiny splashed her nose into the water and pawed it with her foot.

"Careful, Tiny," I said as I put my hand in to move the water away from her pawing it. Tiny was too fast for me and managed to knock the ketchup lid over before I could stop her.

"Right, I might try that in the corner next time," I told Tiny. I refilled the ketchup lid in the bathroom and placed it carefully in the corner.

"You okay up there, Lilly? You keep running to the bathroom!" yelled Mum.

I wondered if Uncle Joe had been messaging her on his phone.

"I'm fine, Mum, just hanging out in my room."

Food was a tricky one. The ponies at the riding school got hay in the stables, and grass in the fields. They also got a bucket feed at night when they were all tucked up for the evening. Holly had said to me, "Put the feed buckets over their doors before you leave. You must make sure the horse gets the right feed with its name on the bucket. It's really important how we make them up as if some of the feed doesn't get soaked before you give them to the horses, they can get sick." I wished I had asked Holly what exactly it was that they ate and what needed to be soaked at the time. "I don't want to give you hamster food or anything, Tiny, cos if I feed you the wrong thing it could make you sick. Maybe I can ask Kalila what she feeds her horse and where she gets it from tomorrow. I'll get you some grass, though."

I went downstairs and into the garden. Mum had not mowed the lawn in ages. She loved to let it grow for the wildlife and bees. I picked some handfuls and snuck the grass into my pocket. I went to the fridge and saw little carrot batons that I got for my packed lunch. I sneaked one out.

"What are you taking from the fridge?" Mum asked me.

"Just a quick snack, Mum."

I put the kettle on and thought I would take her through a cup of tea to the living room while I was down there. It always puts her in a good mood, and she would ask fewer questions.

"Why not grab a packet of raisins?" I wished we could just buy crisps like normal people but apparently not only were raisins healthier they came in recyclable cardboard things instead of plastic packets.

"I'll take some carrots if that's okay."

"Even better," said Mum.

I finished making Mum's cup of tea. The trick was to only fill it three quarters, so I didn't get it on my hand taking it through to the living room—Rebecca taught me that. She was good at common sense things. I put it down in front of Mum and she looked up and smiled.

"That's sweet, Lilly. What has brought this on? Are you hoping to talk me round for that show at the weekend?"

"I was just making you a cup of tea, Mum. I would love to go, though." I could sneak Tiny there in my pocket and let her see other horses so she would have pony friends.

"Aw, I love a cup of tea that someone else has made for me. Are you sure you don't want anything?"

"No. Can I borrow your phone, though, to call Rebecca?"

"Yeah okay, bring it back when you're finished."

I ran up to my room with Mum's phone and put the carrot and grass in Tiny's stable. Tiny looked truly excited at the addition of the carrot baton to her cage. She chewed with such enthusiasm. I smiled, watching her enjoyment.

I kicked off my shoes and called Rebecca's mobile. "Hey, Rebecca. It's me."

"Yeah, I guessed that when your mum's number came up."

"What are you up to?"

"I'm just chilling; I had my karate class tonight. I've got a lot of my stuff packed up now so I'm not bothering with the science homework stuff. I'll probably be away by then, anyway."

"I'm gonna miss you so much. I don't know who I'll have lunch with when you go."

"Louise and her crowd are nice. Ask to sit at their lunch table," said Rebecca.

"I tried that when you were off sick once and Natasha and Erin came over and were just totally embarrassing, so I left," I said.

"You should have stayed. Louise is quite sweet, and she can't be bothered with all the bitching. She pulled Natasha's hair at school camp when she tried to put water in her bed, so I don't think she worries too much about what Natasha has to say." Rebecca said.

"Always something I liked about Louise. Maybe she can give me lessons in pulling Natasha's hair," I said.

We laughed, allies against the bullies, not having to explain that I was only joking. I'm not going to pull anyone's hair or be told that I just need to speak up. As if it's my fault for not speaking up rather than Natasha's fault for being mean.

"Can you bring me some hay and straw from your hamster stuff tomorrow?"

"Yeah, no worries. Did your hippy mum get you a hamster and forget to get you the feed and bedding for it?"

"Well, it's kinda like a tiny little pony but it's hamster sized. It's amazing." I couldn't keep a secret from Rebecca once I heard her voice. "Her name is Tiny and she's so, so cute."

"You're nuts, Lilly, you and your pony obsession. But your hamster can be a pony if you want it to be."

"No, it really is. Video chat me and I'll show you" I told her.

"Rebecca, get off that phone and get your clothes sorted out into piles of coming and not coming," came an adult's voice from the background of Rebecca's phone. "Rebecca, I sent you up here to do it over an hour ago and you haven't even started. Give me that phone... Hi Lilly, sorry, I'm taking Rebecca's phone for the rest of this evening as we have so much to do before we move, and she's been sitting here chatting. We'll have you over at the new place for a sleepover once we are settled in, okay, sweetie?"

"Yes please, thank you, Mrs. McGregor."

"I hope Rebecca brings it tomorrow as I think she's unsure whether I have a hamster or am just joking with her. I sure know she doesn't believe me about you right now. Maybe just as well," I told Tiny.

Ten

Chapter 10

Now I had all the things that Tiny needed. I picked her up and brought her onto my bed with me. Tiny came running up into my lap. I looked through an old toy box I had hidden under the bed and found an old action figure, with her own horse, and grooming kit. I had to dig to the bottom of the box as all the little brushes from the kit had fallen out and were right at the bottom.

I remember the morning that I got it one Christmas. I was so excited when I saw the gift. The box it came in had big red printing saying "Pony in My Pocket - with real miniature scale working saddle and bridle." It also had a book on pony care that came with it, that was now sitting on my bookshelf with juice spilt on it from my night-time reads. I remembered the joy when I saw it, and a younger me had played with the little rider and her pony for hours, with me pretending that I was the rider.

"Come back on my lap, Tiny, I'm all sorted now," I told her.

Tiny came over to see her new horsey friend on my lap. "It's just a toy from when I was a kid, but you can play with it if you like," I told her.

I used the little brushes to groom her mane. All the mud from the field fell out and it puffed up all pretty and full as I brushed it. I worked on her coat next and tried to remember what Kalila had told me about grooming. She had a much bigger grooming kit for Chintzy than I had for Tiny. Not just in brush size, but all the different types of brushes she had too. I gently ran a brush along with Tiny's coat, and she gazed happily at me. "You're just loving that, aren't you, Tiny?"

Tiny nickered to tell me of her approval.

Such an affectionate little pony, she must have been craving all this fuss for a long time. When I came to do her tail, it was so knotted and thick with mud I was scared I'd hurt her. I pulled out my detangling spray and a shampoo and hair conditioner bottle from the bathroom and coated her tail. I used my fingers to massage the thick white goop from the shampoo bottle all the way through and right into all the matted tangles watching my fingers turn murky brown with soapy bubbles. The mud felt cold and clumpy on my fingers. It took a few goes of rinsing the shampoo from Tiny's tail in the bathroom sink before it was time to go back to my bedroom for the conditioner. I looked at the bottle which said *Coconut Conditioner for Thick Hair*. I thought that would be perfect for Tiny's thick tail, so I opened the bottle and took a sniff. Tiny was already smelling a whole lot better from shampooing and brushing out her tail. She seemed to appreciate it so she stood nicely as I enjoyed the fresh coconut aroma, massaging it well into her tail before combing it through as I sat on my bed with a towel over the duvet to catch any pony washing clues from being left behind. The top of her tail wasn't just the hair, it was actually like a dog's tail at the top just covered in so much hair that you couldn't see it. I knew from Holly that this was called the dock and would be able to feel temperature and stuff, so I was glad I had used tepid water.

Tiny was beginning to look less raggedy by the minute. This tatty little scruffy pony had more prettiness revealed with every brush. I suppose that all ponies are beautiful, but Tiny was extra special to me. As I worked away at her tail being gentle while still getting as much muck as possible out of it.

Tiny's little tail was amazing when it was all brushed out. I turned back to her body and coat and wondered what to do to finish off cleaning her up. I stayed sitting on my bed and pulled the towel over my lap and stood her on for ease of grooming. I had a little dandy brush like the kind that Kalila had used on Chintzy to groom her coat. Tiny's black glossy prettiness, so shiny it looked as though there was silver sparkle, started to appear in bigger and bigger patches as the clumps of brown mud became smaller, and I worked over her coat.

Tiny had dried off a fair bit but a few bits of mud had dried back in, but it was fun to enjoy brushing those last bits away and seeing it being replaced by a shiny healthy coat. It was a good job that Tiny loved getting brushed and cleaned up. Her little feet pressed gently in my leg as she wandered about my lap, nudging me with her nose to brush her. We were both so lost in the moment that all my mind was taken up with just enjoying hanging out with my own little special pony. As tiny as she was in height didn't stop her feeling large in my heart.

"Oh, you are showing me how lovely your tail is," I said to Tiny as she suddenly lifted her tail. It looked so beautiful as I admired the pretty black rush of thick hair, bright and striking, long and luscious. Just as I was admiring the polished beauty of her much cleaner tail, several round balls of poop came out from under it and fell onto my lap. I should have seen that coming!

"It's a good job I'm used to pony poop, Tiny." I brushed the poop into my hand and tried to lean over and pop it into my wastebasket in the corner of my room. Not leaning too far forward though when I had a precious pony on my lap. I missed the basket and the poop fell to the floor, but a little horse manure didn't bother me. I asked Tiny, "I wonder if I could house train you like people house train puppies or kittens?"

I was in awe of how lovely Tiny now was and felt more than a little proud of how her makeover had spruced her up. I didn't just have a pony of my own now; I had a beautiful pony, and I couldn't believe my luck. The joy of her smallness meant I could keep her secret and not have anyone ever take her from me. Just me and Tiny. A team forever.

"Wanna play now you are all beautiful?" I asked Tiny.

Tiny answered by running to the foot of the bed and back up onto my lap again.

"I wonder if you know how to be ridden. Have you had a rider before?" I picked the toy horse up from earlier and took the saddle and bridle off it. A chestnut-coloured plastic pony, I think it was meant to be an Arab, with its plastic tail held high in the air, its head held high, and feet fixed into position as though it was trotting. I put the plastic toy horse onto the bed next to me and Tiny came running over and gave it a sniff. "Hey Tiny, now you have a friend. I used to play with this toy pony all the time when I was younger." Tiny stood back and watched the plastic horse suspiciously as though she was waiting for it to sniff her back. I was pleased she had a new friend but I didn't think the plastic pony was going to move around and play galloping games with her as much as she might like. I found it super adorable that Tiny was trying to groom the plastic pony with her teeth, wanting to make friends. They were the same size at least.

As I decided the plastic toy pony wouldn't mind, I took its saddle and bridle off. I knew that there had been instructions in the book on how to put a saddle and bridle on and off. With my tips from Holly and having read the instructions over many times, I knew exactly what to do to put the saddle and bridle onto Tiny. I wasn't sure that she would let me but as it turned out she was happy enough to get the saddle and bridle on. I was a little worried that with the pony being made of plastic, the metal bit in the bridle would be plastic and not be safe to go in Tiny's mouth. A toy saddle and bridle from a toy pony might not work on Tiny with her being real. I felt the bit with my fingertips and the cold smooth feel let me know it was indeed metal. Both the saddle and the bridle seemed to be a little big at first so I adjusted the buckles the way Holly had shown me until eventually the saddle and bridle seemed to fit Tiny perfectly as though they had been made especially for her. I wondered if Holly met Tiny and if she would like her. I bet she would. I imagined Holly seeing Tiny and admiring how lovely she was and that she would want to give me riding lessons on her and let me go for hacks with the other girls.

Now Tiny had her tack on and was looking happy, so I picked up the doll that came with the plastic horse. The riding hat was already on the doll, and she had lost a shoe. "Okay, Tiny, let's see if you can take a rider. I think I might be a bit big for you, but this doll might be okay. At least if you buck her off, she won't get hurt."

I gently moved the doll towards Tiny and let her have a sniff. I slowly moved the doll onto Tiny, and she stood there calmly as I put the doll's little feet into the stirrups. The doll's hands were fixed so they could hold the reins, so I popped the reins into her little fingers. Tiny stood nicely and I pretended I was leading her the way I led the riders in the lessons that Holly taught.

I remembered what Holly had shown me about checking the girth and stirrup leathers and how to do the fancy buckles. My tongue stayed in my mouth when doing this despite being absorbed in what I was doing, as I began to feel I was getting the hang of these things. I suppose it was easier knowing that if I got it wrong Tiny would never laugh at me.

Tiny looked so proud of herself that she had a job. She walked around the bed with her head raised, picking her feet up, showing me how proud she was of carrying her doll rider. I walked Tiny around with a little toy lead rope that came with the plastic horse, while the rider stayed on her back and I saw her enjoyment at being ridden. I led Tiny a little faster and when she sprang into a bouncy sweet trot making the little doll jiggle up and down so much! I giggled watching them prancing around and loved how cute the super small pony trot that Tiny had as she pranced around my bed.

"Oh Tiny, I don't have a doll that knows rising trot so we will have to go with sitting," I said, but they both seemed happy enough.

I put Tiny in my little hamster obstacle course. "Let's see if you can take the doll around that course." I didn't know whether Tiny understood me, but she certainly had seen a course of jumps before and knew just what to do. She went cantering off over the first jump and took off, jumping twice the height she needed to. The doll fell off as Tiny landed from the jump, as being a rigid plastic doll she couldn't bend and move with the horse like the showjumpers I had seen on TV. Tiny didn't seem too bothered and carried on anyway to the next one. The doll lay abandoned in the course as Tiny ran from one jump to the next, leaping over them.

"You can stop now, your doll's fallen off," I told Tiny, but she was having such a ball that she kept running around anyway. By the end of the course, I was very impressed she hadn't knocked any down. "No faults; clever little Tiny," I told her.

Mum came into my room and saw my doll and toy horse lying around. "Hey, it's been a while since I've seen you playing with your dolls. Or is this your science project? With the hamster course? You're determined you're getting the hamster, aren't you Lilly?"

Oh no! What if she looked in the hamster course?

"Hmmm, maybe I've gone off the idea, maybe a bag of horse feed would be nice," I told her.

"Is this about the ponies in the field near Uncle Joe's that the farmer has that are going, Lilly?" Mum came in and sat on my bed. She always did that when I was trying to get rid of her from my room. "It's very sweet that you're so caring but you know that you can't save everything."

I tried to think fast of a way of distracting Mum, terrified that she would look in my hamster course and discover my wonderful glossy black real-life secret.

"I know," I said.

Mum turned to look at the pile of toys strewn about and said, "I thought you were a bit old for all this stuff. It's nice to see you have it all out again. I'm glad we didn't throw it all away."

I grabbed my opportunity to bend down to pick the toy horse off the ground. At the same time, I sneakily collected Tiny out of her hamster course with my other hand and put her in my pocket.

Phew, that was close!

I could feel Tiny wriggling around in my pocket. I wished my mum would leave. "Everything okay at school, Lilly?"

Tiny wriggled some more, and I stroked her, hoping that she would be still.

"I know you built all this for a hamster that you're wanting, but I don't think it's good for me to teach you that this pressuring me will get you your own way. I mean, it starts off with a hamster, but you also want a dog, a kitten and of course a pony. If it was up to you we would need a zoo."

"It's okay, Mum, I've gone off the idea of a hamster."

"What, so you're going to just nag about the kitten, the dog and the pony now?" Mum laughed.

"Yeah, well maybe a little." I made a small gap between my thumb and index finger and showed the small space between them to my mum.

Eleven

Chapter 11

Once it was time for bed, I brought Tiny in beside me. I felt the warm snuggliness of fabric softener scented pyjamas enjoying the soft comfiness surrounding me. I loved fleecy pyjamas. I thought about getting a soft sock and cutting holes in it so Tiny could poke her legs through and have her own pyjamas, but I thought she might be used to it being much colder outside. I had read a few magazine articles on picking the right rug out for a horse in my pony magazines. I knew it was worse to have them over rugged than a little chilly for their health, so I decided against the homemade sock rug, even though it would have been so cute.

When I brought Tiny into my bed, I made a little tent with the duvet for her and me so if Mum came in, she couldn't see my pony. I had brought a little torch under the covers with me, as I wasn't sure if ponies were scared of the dark or not. I knew Tiny was used to being in a dark field at night normally, but inside dark can be scarier than outside dark.

"Hey little cutie, so this is different from your field. Do you like under the covers with me, or do you want to be on top of the covers and sleep on the bed like a dog? Shall I read you a story?"

I loved having my very own pony. It didn't matter that Tiny was small and had to be a secret or that even Rebecca didn't believe me. Having my own special little pony to cuddle up to at night made it feel as if all my dreams had come true. I had such a feeling of contentment and got sleepier and sleepier while I stroked Tiny's coat. Tiny lay down beside me and closed her eyes and drifted lazily off to sleep, my mind full of thoughts of all the fun we would have together.

Mum flicked my light on as she called out, "Morning Lilly, time to get up," and closed the door again. I started to come around a bit and peeled the covers back to find Tiny. She should still be curled up, snoozing away. I imagined she wouldn't be up and rushing about getting ready because it's not like Tiny has school to worry about. I thought Tiny's normal routine was much more likely a busy schedule of eating grass and hanging out in a field full instead of rushing about to make the school bell.

Where was Tiny? I looked where she had curled up in our little under duvet tent and all under the covers and couldn't find her. The soft pillows squished as I frantically threw them on the floor to see if she had crawled under them.

"Ewwwww!" I heard Mum squeal from the hall.

"Are you okay, Mum?"

Oh no, Mum was having a problem and where was Tiny? I began to panic and pulled the duvet right off the bed to see if I had missed where she could be lying. What if I had squished Tiny during the night?

I pulled my duvet cover off the duvet in case Tiny had climbed inside there. I could hear Mum shouting, "Mice, mice, we have mice!"

I went running, terrified that she had found Tiny first. "Hey, Mum, what do you mean, mice?"

"I'm gonna stamp on it as soon as I find it, definitely a mouse in here!"

"Er, did you see it, Mum? What colour was the mouse?"

"No Lilly, I've just stood in a pile of its poo. Mice poo all over the hall! And now all over the soles of my feet!"

Mum pointed at lots of little droppings all up and down the hallway, except they weren't mice droppings, they were like little apples of manure, like what a tiny, small pony would make. Tiny. At least I knew now that I hadn't squashed her while I had been sleeping.

"How many times have I told you not to eat snacks in your bedroom? Now you have attracted a mouse into the house, and we need to kill it!"

"Mum, calm down, it's just a really small animal. I never knew you were so... murdery."

"But they're vermin. They carry so much disease. If you have one mouse, you have a family of mice, and they breed so quickly."

"Maybe we could just find the mouse? And put it outside?"

"You can't touch them and pick them up. We need to call an exterminator to kill them."

OMG, I didn't want her to exterminate my Tiny.

"They can lay traps and poison."

I was in such a panic I almost forgot Mum's one soft spot. "What effect does all that poison have on the environment, Mum? Is it eco-friendly?"

Mum's voice was still high pitched as a look of realisation came across her face. "Oh yes, good point, Lilly! I'll phone Mag's next door and ask her if she can pop the cat in when we are out at work and school. That's much more natural. Mother nature always has a better way with these things."

NOOOOOOOOOOOOOOOOOO!

"Er, Mum, why don't we just leave them be—like part of our ecosystem and all that."

"Yeah, well that won't be happening," said Mum as she pulled her phone out of her pocket and called Mags from next door.

Mum wandered downstairs and started chattering to Mags, so I went back into my room and called, "Tiny, Tiny, don't be scared. Please come out." There was silence.

I looked in the toy box, under my chest of drawers, in the hamster course, in the back of the wardrobe, everywhere. I was still looking when Mum came back upstairs. "Lilly, why aren't you dressed yet? You're always making us late. And why has your lunch box got lots of holes stabbed in it? Why are your pillows and bedding all over the place? Are you just trying to make my life harder?" Her voice getting higher and louder and her face giving me that Angry Mum look...oh, crap. I think the mouse stress was pushing her over the edge this morning.

"Mum, I don't feel well. Can't I stay at home today?" I couldn't go to school and leave Mags' cat to murder my sweet Tiny. It could be the end of the happy time we were due to have together. It would be too cruel to have worked out how to shrink her, save her from the farmer, and have next door's cat eat her for lunch, but I couldn't see any other way that this was going to go.

Mum walked over to me and put her hand on my forehead. "You feel fine, now stop messing about. I've had it with your nonsense today. I have a big day at work, a really important meeting first thing, and you're doing everything you can to make me late for it."

Do mums actually think we work that way; that we wake up in the morning and think, "just to be a pain? I think I'll make my mum late?". And I am the one being babyish. Ooommmphhh. I pushed my lips together and felt my annoyance and fear rise on the inside.

I didn't argue back in the hope my mum would stop all this nonsense, but she carried on. "If I end up getting sacked because of you, who's going to pay the mortgage, the magical mortgage fairy?

Maybe they can keep the car on the road too? It's been making grating sounds a lot on the corners lately, I could use a mortgage and car fixing fairy right now."

I grabbed the school uniform out of my drawers and kept looking around my room as I got ready. I had to find Tiny before I left so she wouldn't be cat food.

Mum called up the stairs, "Hurry! Hurry! Hurry!"

I hauled my school uniform on ultra-fast and kept hunting around my room. No wonder Tiny didn't want to come back with all Mum's shouting and carrying on this morning. "Please Tiny, please come, I can't leave you here loose." I continued searching.

Mum shouted up the stairs, "Lilly, I haven't even heard you visit the bathroom yet. We don't have time for breakfast now, just get your teeth done and get in the car."

I ran to the bathroom and put the tap on as full and loud as it would go. "Tiny, Tiny!" I called out.

I thought I heard something from under the bath and moved the bath panel to peek behind it. "Tiny!"

"Parp!" I heard the noise again. I froze still to hear better and when the noise came the third time, I realised it was the radiator making noises.

Gutted, I tried to figure a way of getting more time to hunt for her. I ran to my room and continued looking everywhere. Ten minutes later, Mum appeared and took me by the arm. "Lilly, car, now." She marched me out to the car and then she went to Mags'.

Mag was already in her dressing gown and standing in her open front doorway.

"That girl is full of silliness this morning, Mags. Don't know what's up with her. There's the front door key. If you even can just pop the cat in for a couple of hours that would be grand."

The tears were pooling up in my eyes as I tried to figure out what to do. Should I escape from school and try to climb in a window? What if I was too late and Tiny was already eaten? Should I tell Mum the truth and hope she believed me? Or just face Mum's wrath and pretend I snuck a hamster into the house?"

I looked out. Raindrops were beginning to fall against the car window as well as drops beginning to come down from my eyes. I felt as if the sky was crying with me. I wiped my tears away and sniffed hard. I didn't want to cry when I was dropped off at school. Then I looked up at Mum's bedroom window.

Standing on the windowsill, tucked behind the curtain, out of sight, was Tiny. She casually perched on the windowsill happily chewing on Mum's aloe vera plant. "Tiny!"

I jumped out of the car and ran to Mum. "Mum, I need the key. I forgot something."

"I'm actually going to kill you, Lilly! Whatever it is can wait. We need to leave now. We have run out of time."

Twelve

Chapter 12

"But I forgot my gym kit. Please, I'll be straight in and out. Please let me go in and get it."

Mum sighed so deeply it was as though she was weighing things up. Instead of deciding to commit a child murder and spending the next twenty years in jail, she must have weighed things up in my favour. She handed me the key and said, "Oh Mags, it's so hard trying to be a superhero in the workplace and supermum at home."

Thank goodness she's not shouting at me, I thought as I took the key and ran into the house.

I ran up the stairs so fast that I fell and bumped my knee and just kept running, pulling back the curtain in Mum's room, and there she was.

"Oh Tiny, you are far too good for your own sake at hide and seek. You have no idea how close you were to being eaten by the cat next door."

I picked up Tiny and popped her in my pocket, went to my room and picked up some carrot batons, yesterday's lunch box and all the brushes and accessories for little Tiny. I placed it all in one of the reusable bags from the kitchen so Mum would think it was my gym kit until I got it into my school bag. I ran back to Mum with the key.

"Where's your gym kit?"

"Right here."

"Huuuuuuhhhhhhh." came a rush of breath from mum's chest. Mum's sighs were major when she was annoyed. In fact, if sighing was an Olympic sport I would say that when stressed out my mum could definitely compete for Great Britain. "Okay, Mags, I'd better get going. There's the key. Thanks for this, I'll see you tonight."

"No problem, see you when you're in from work. I'll do a check and remove any mice corpses I can see when I bring my cat out."

"You're a star, Mags, don't know what I would do without you," Mum replied as she climbed in the car and closed the door.

"Lilly, why are you late again? Hurry up and take your seat."

That frustrating feeling when you try your best to be good and just get in trouble all the time was becoming more familiar to me.

"Sorry, Mrs Brown."

I ran and took my seat at my new table even though I wanted to sit next to Rebecca. Best to not try it on when I am already in trouble, I thought. I looked at Rebecca and gave her my best, "Meet me in the toilet at the break," look. Rebecca saw and gave me back a look that said "Ok, see you there."

"Stop fidgeting," Natasha hissed at me as I tried to comfort little Tiny in my pocket.

I looked down at my work and hoped she would move on to someone else soon.

"You're such a child, so distracting," she went on.

Will break time ever come? I wondered. But you know how it is when you're desperate for school to end. The more you have something good after school and want the day to go quickly, the slower it goes. As soon as the bell went for the first break, I headed for the loo, the last cubicle, and waited for Rebecca's special knock.

"Hey, sorry about last night with Mum, she's so crabbit with the move and everything," Rebecca said as she came into the cubicle. It was a bit squashy for two, but we always made it work.

"That's ok. I know what it's like when Mums are stressed. Well, my Mum anyway...." I reassured her.

Rebecca explained, "The moving vans are coming on Saturday morning, but my Mum still said I had to come to school as if *I* was the one that was behaving nuts."

"I need to show you something. Get your back to the door," I told her excitedly.

Rebecca turned and put her back against the toilet door and said, "Why are we meeting in here anyway? What did you want to tell me? Did I tell you my new room is going to be pink...*pink* for me? I swear my mum's been trying to get me to be all girly and dress-wearing since I told her when I grew up, I wanted to marry another girl and it's just—"

Rebecca was never speechless, but her words suddenly stopped as I pulled out Tiny and held her in the palm of my hand.

"Wow, Lilly, that looks so real, and it's moving! Where did you get that? OMG, it's real!"

Rebecca put her finger out and stroked Tiny's side. "But how? Where did you get it?"

"I know. I love her, Rebecca. She's my very own teeny tiny pony," I told her. I looked at her mouth agape and eyes wide and saw she loved Tiny too. Even if she wasn't normally a horsey girl this was different; Tiny was special.

Rebecca took her apple out of her trouser pocket and bit off a chunk that she dropped into her fingers. She put the piece of apple towards Tiny, offering it. Tiny took a step forward and sniffed the apple, not quite trusting it to be sweet, tasty food until she had thoroughly investigated it. Once it had passed Tiny's inspection, she decided to greedily crunch on it, clearly enjoying herself.

"Oh, she's so cute. She's munching the bit of apple, it's huge to her. I thought you were joking on the phone. I thought you meant a hamster....and that you were pretending to yourself it was a pony. I thought it was just you being weird."

"It's the best thing that's ever happened to me. You need to stay now and enjoy this secret with me," I told her.

Bang! I heard the main entrance door to the toilets bang shut.

"What secret?" Erin's voice travelled over the toilet cubicle.

"Get knotted!" shouted Rebecca back over the cubicle door.

I popped Tiny back into my pocket. I heard the door being banged around as Rebecca continued to lean against it, maybe putting a little more weight on it. I saw Natasha's head pop over the door.

"Oh, my God, is that your secret? Speccy Lilly's in the toilets with Rebecca the big fat monster...hahahahaha!" She began to sing, "Lilly and Rebecca...up a tree!"

Erin joined in and they chanted together "K-I-S-S-I-N-G, first comes the aaaarrrrgggghhhh!" Natasha couldn't finish the song as Rebecca swung the door open and Natasha fell down off the door.

"I'll give you a big fat punch!" Rebecca shouted at Natasha as she landed from the door on the floor.

Natasha stood up and moved close to Rebecca's face and shoved her in the centre of her chest.

"You shouldn't have been kissing in the toilets then. I'm telling on you for that and for throwing me on the floor."

I didn't even have time to wonder what a big fat punch would be like, but as it turns out they are pretty similar to other big punches.

Rebecca drew back her arm and swung it forward as her fist made a thudding sound against Natasha's cheek.

Erin turned and opened the door to the toilets to make her escape and ran away with Natasha trying to run and follow her. Natasha wasn't fast enough for Rebecca who grabbed her by the sweater and told her, "See your smart mouth...keep it to yourself. Your bullying and nasty comments had better stop. We have all had enough!".

As soon as she released Natasha's jumper, she ran for the door, but she wasn't out it fast enough as Rebecca kicked her right on the butt, like in a cartoon. Natasha lurched forward with the force of the thrust but stayed on her feet and continued to run up the hallway with Erin, shouting "Teachers!!!" as she went.

"Rebecca, I wish I had your guts. I never know the right thing to say."

"I didn't know what to say either. That's why I punched her. What are they gonna do? keep me back for detention from to-morrow on when I won't be here? Tell my mum who is cross all the time just now anyway?"

This was why Rebecca was my friend. She wasn't just great at not taking crap from anyone, but she was so clever too.

"I've been wanting to do that for ages anyway," said Rebecca.

Mrs Zanya, the head teacher, came running in.

"Right girls, I've just heard you have been attacking other girls in here. I've seen poor Natasha's lip. That's the end of the break for you. My office, now."

Whenever I was in trouble, I always got this sick, thudding feeling in my chest. The feeling of exhilaration from watching Natasha run away instead of picking on me was gone and was replaced with a feeling of dread.

What if the school phoned my mum to come and get me and I was banned from the riding school night tonight? If I missed it, I wouldn't be able to find out more about pony care from Kalila. Now that I had Tiny to think about, learning about pony care was essential. Mum would ban me from going out and give me one of these shouting acts that lasted forever. My mum could turn giving rows into an all-evening event when I did something really bad. I suppose hitting someone would be considered in the really bad category. Even if it wasn't even me, Natasha started it, and she deserved it. Oh, the unfairness. And there was not even any point in trying to explain it as Natasha and Erin would always be found sweet and innocent. That's how it worked when your parents were in the Parent-Teacher Association at my school.

Once in her room, Mrs Zanya sat looking straight at me and Rebecca.

"Right, what happened?"

"Natasha climbed the toilet and called me a big fat monster, said I was kissing in the toilets, so I opened the door and she fell off. Then she shoved me, and I hit her," Rebecca told her matter-of-factly before continuing "I also grabbed her jumper while I told her to stop bullying and when I let her go, I kicked her bum when she ran away."

"For goodness sake. I find it hard to believe Natasha would call anyone such a thing, and it's not the first time you have hit someone. We have a *no mean hands* policy in this school. I am putting a note in both your school bags for your parents to see and until they come to see me, you will both spend all break times and lunch in the detention room. I can't have bullying in this school."

"It was Natasha that shoved me first and it was me that hit her back, and it was an accident she fell off the door when I swung it open. I did mean to kick her up the butt when she ran away though. So why is Lilly in trouble?"

"Because both the girls explained that you both hit them and pulled them off the door. I wasn't there but I can't have you pair hitting people in the toilets. We just won't put up with that," she firmly told us.

I looked up from my shoes to Mrs Zanya. The unfairness of it all! I had to say something. "But we are not the bullies. Natasha is always—"

"Did Natasha or Erin hit either of you in the toilet, Lilly?"

"No, but—"

"Well then, it's quite clear, so I will see you both in the detention room at lunch. You can sit here until the bell."

I looked awkwardly at my shoes. I glanced up at Rebecca. She looked as if she didn't care. That's because she didn't. At least I would have lunchtime alone with Rebecca without Erin and Natasha's smart comments. It made me glad that Rebecca had gotten rid of Natasha and glad Rebecca didn't seem to care about the trouble she was in. I looked up and smiled at her and she caught my eye and smiled back.

Mrs Zanya looked up and we looked away, pretending we hadn't been looking at each other. Back in the classroom after the break, sitting between Erin and Natasha would have been unbearable if I hadn't had my Tiny with me in my pocket. Erin stamped on my foot hard under the table and hissed,

"See how smart you are when Rebecca's not here, ugly speccy face."

Ignoring them, I managed to work through art, maths, and science and waited for lunch to come. If teachers thought it through, they wouldn't put you in detention with your friends. I would much rather be with Rebecca in the warm detention room than outside anyway. And if no other kids had detention, I could have Tiny out again. I actually couldn't wait for detention.

I felt in my pocket to stroke Tiny as I was sure that she had fallen asleep. There was no longer any wriggling in my pocket, and she had been staying still for quite a while, but my hand just moved around my pocket. Empty. Huh?

I checked my other pocket. Empty. I looked under the table. Nothing. Oh no. I scanned my eyes under the table. I looked at Rebecca, but she had her head down writing in her jotter. I climbed under the table and looked around.

"Mrs Brown, Lilly is under the table." Natasha's voice grated whenever I heard it.

"Lilly, what are you doing under there? Get in your seat now."

I looked and saw Tiny standing hiding under Mrs Brown's table.

If I went and got her now, everyone would see. I looked at Rebecca and explained the problem to her using my eyes in the way that only best friends can.

I sat in my seat and saw Rebecca get out of her seat and go over to the teacher's desk. I didn't want her looking at Rebecca, so I stood up in my chair and turned around pretending to look for something, getting Mrs Brown's attention off Rebecca.

"Lilly, what are you doing? Sit down?" I looked over at Rebecca and she was by Mrs Brown's desk, but she didn't have Tiny yet.

I spun around weirdly another couple of times as it was all I could think to do.

"Lilly, sit down now! What is wrong with you today!" she scolded. I spied Rebecca out of the corner of my eye as she put her jotter on the desk and bent down to scoop up little Tiny.

Mrs Brown was still distracted from telling me off. "For goodness sake, aren't you in enough trouble today?"

I sat in my seat not even caring about the telling off from the teacher, knowing that Rebecca would keep hold of Tiny until lunchtime detention for me. Hurry up detention, I thought, I'm ready for you.

Thirteen

Chapter 13

The bell went and off I headed for the detention classroom where Mrs Zanya stood. "Right, you two, I've some marking to do, but I will be back to check that you are both behaving." She turned and left, the door making a banging sound.

We sat on the floor together and made a diamond shape with our legs, our legs both stretched out and the soles of our feet touching. I put Tiny in the middle of our leg diamond, pulled the lettuce out of my lunch sandwich, and placed it on the floor.

"That's sooooo cute, the way she's running over for the lettuce. What are you going to do with her, Lilly?"

"I don't know, just love her I guess."

Rebecca put her bottle top on the floor and filled it with water from her bottle. "Come and get a drink, little one." Tiny wandered over to the bottle top and drank away. "Oh, look at her! I thought you were kidding me with the tiny pony thing. Look in my school bag though, I do have the hay and straw and hamster foodstuff you asked me to bring."

I knew she wouldn't let me down.

I was stuffing Rebecca's emergency tiny pony supply kit of hay, straw and hamster food into my bag and Tiny went back over to munch the remaining lettuce. "So, nobody else knows about this, Lilly? How did it happen?"

"You know Uncle Joe and how he likes inventing stuff? Kinda that's how."

"Your Uncle Joe knows?" she asked as I pulled the accessories I had for Tiny out of my bag. I shook my head.

"Really Lilly? So, nobody else knows?" She kept chatting as I pulled out the little brush and started brushing Tiny's tail.

I handed Rebecca the dandy brush so that she could join in with the grooming.

"I don't want anyone to take her away or say I can't have her. My mum said no to a hamster! I really can't see her agreeing to the world's only two-inch horse!"

Rebecca was plaiting Tiny's tail now and I was scratching her front shoulder.

"Look, she loves it so much when you scratch her. She pulls funny faces." I looked at the silly faces that Tiny was pulling and burst out laughing.

Munching our sandwiches, minus the lettuce, of course, we fussed away at Tiny until she was plaited up and looking amazing.

I showed her the saddle and bridle that I had and explained to her "Do you remember us playing with this at my house when we were in our first year at school? How proud I was as it had a proper saddle scaled down to size so I could play with all the bits like the stirrup leathers and girth?"

"Trust you to have doll ponies with saddles and bridles to fit, that's so cool," Rebecca told me as Tiny trotted around showing off her saddle and bridle. "Do you think she can be ridden, if you manage to make yourself super small too, Lilly?"

"Yeah, I think so, I had one of my old dolls from when I was a kid lying around and Tiny seemed fine carrying her about. I think she's had a rider before from her reaction."

Tiny came over to sniff to check I was still me and she snuggled her face against my hand. She stretched her back legs out behind her. "What is she doing, is she trying to do the splits or some kind of strange horse yoga?" Rebecca asked.

Tiny responded by maintaining her strange stretched back leg position and started doing a pee. It was an enormous pee for such a small pony. The pee went all over the hard lino floor and the puddle spread quite a distance, all along with the diamond shape that we had made with our legs to keep Tiny safe. We moved our legs to stop them from getting wet, and I scooped Tiny up and put her into my pocket, just as the door swung open.

Mrs Zanya popped her head through the door.

"What are you two doing down there? You shouldn't be lying around on the floor, get up! Good grief, what's the puddle? It smells like urine. Has one of you wet yourself?"

Rebecca sucked her cheeks in to stop herself from laughing. "Yeah miss, it happens all the time. Had a bit of a sore tummy today."

"Oh, I see, well you'd best go down and see the nurse. She can phone your mum if you're not well."

I could hardly keep my laughter in. I kept my eyes down, knowing if I just glanced in Rebecca's direction, I would lose all control.

Rebecca continued, "Yeah, I thought I was gonna poop myself as well," and there I went.

The giggles came flying out my mouth. I tried to hide them by coughing, but the laugh came out over the top.

"Lilly, laughing at someone having such an embarrassing incident is very unkind. I thought Rebecca was your friend."

The laughter came and didn't stop coming. Every time I tried to get the laugh to stop, I pictured Rebecca's serious face when she announced that she had in fact wet herself and there was nothing I could do to push my laugh down.

"Right, that's enough. Rebecca, you go to the nurse's office and get sorted out. Since Lilly finds this so hilarious, she can get a mop and bucket from the janitor and clean up."

It was totally worth the telling off, and for the rest of the day, every time the incident came into my mind, I couldn't stop smirking and had to suppress some giggles. The janitor told me I wasn't allowed to clean it up for health and safety anyway.

Rebecca was always clever; now she was being sent home sick, her detention was all forgotten about, and she had the rest of the day off. And she wouldn't be here for any detention tomorrow or any day after that. I thought I was just going to have to stay in every lunch rather than give my mum the letter. It would be better than sitting alone in the lunch area when Rebecca left anyway.

When we got back to our classroom, I thought I best take no more chances of escaping ponies. Tiny was turning into quite the escape artist so with her back in the lunchbox with holes I kept her in the top of my school bag and peeked in every so often to check she was still there and happy enough.

"Why are you looking in that bag all the time? Natasha said, looking over and trying to peek inside my backpack.

I zipped it back up quickly and said "Nothing," and pretended to be looking at my jotter.

"That bell is due to ring and when it goes off, I'm gonna get you back! Outside! I'm gonna beat you up. I'll kick whatever you have been hiding in that school bag of yours all day right out of the bag and find out whatever you're keeping secret!" Natasha announced.

"Just leave me alone."

"I'm gonna get you back for setting your friend on me, especially now she's been sent homesick."

"But I—"

"*Stop talking!*" shouted Mrs Brown as the school bell rang out.

Fourteen

Chapter 14

I grabbed my bag and ran outside. I ran quickly towards the forest, getting onto the paths that led past the fields and up to Uncle Joe's, hoping that I could get away from Natasha before she beat me up.

I ran along the grass path as it started to swing into a bend and thought I must almost be out of her sight in the distance when I heard Natasha call out, "I'm gonna get you, Lilly!"

I looked behind me and she was in hot pursuit.

"Sorry if this is jostling you, Tiny, but if Natasha and Erin get a hold of me, they will beat me up and stamp on my school bag and I can't have that with you in it."

I saw some thick bushes and jumped into the middle to hide. "Hmmmm," I bit my lip to stop myself from squealing. I thought it might have hurt a bit and was surprised by how sore it was. The thorns from the bushes had scratched right through my clothes. I would check the scratches and lumps and bumps later but at least for now, I was hidden from view a bit inside the bush. Every little movement made another jabby branch brush against me digging into my skin and scratching me. I knew exactly what I had to do. I made big leaps to get to the other side of the bush, so I was hidden from view without the thorns digging into me. I crouched down low so I couldn't be seen. I pulled my bag in front of me and opened the zip as fast as my fumbling panicky fingers would let me. I pulled out my machine from the school bag and took my glasses off and popped them into the machine. I plucked Tiny out and pointed the machine at her with the glasses the same side up as when we had maximised Bessie. She still had her saddle and bridle on from when Rebecca and I had been playing with her. I pressed the button, and nothing happened.

"Where did she go? I can't wait to get her without big mouth Rebecca. She's not fit enough to get that much ahead of us."

I heard Natasha and Erin chatting as they turned the bend and saw all the clear fields and pathways ahead flanked by the thick gorse on either side. They weren't that far, but even if they started checking the thick gorse bushes on either side of the path, there would be a lot to check, so as long as we stayed silent, we might get out of this okay.

I remembered the on/off switch and flicked it on and tried the button again, *whirrr whirr whirr*.

And suddenly Tiny was no longer hidden under the gorse bush with me. She was huge. I quickly threw my machine in my backpack. "Thank goodness your saddle and bridle were left on and zoomed up with you! But I need you to stay still right now."

I put my backpack back on and heard Erin's voice say, "Oh look it's a horse! It's a horse!"

I had always wished to be able to mount from the stirrup like Holly, but I double wished now. I saw a boulder by the bush and led Tiny over. "Please stay still."

"Lilly has stolen the horse, let's take it from her."

They were getting close as I climbed on top of the boulder and put my foot in the stirrup. Now I had to figure out how to get myself from on the boulder to on top of Tiny, and it seemed difficult and scary. I straightened my knee that was in my stirrup thrusting myself upwards into the saddle and luck was on my side as I landed where I wanted to be.

"Please don't buck, please don't buck," I asked her as I landed in the saddle. I wiggled my second foot around and somehow it found the missing stirrup and I pushed my foot in.

"Get off the horse, you don't even have a horse, and you can't ride properly!" The girls were gaining on me, getting closer every second. That was my cue to squeeze my calves around Tiny's sides nudging her on. Tiny bent her neck around turning her face towards me and sniffed my knee as though to check it was definitely me in the saddle. I gave her another little squeeze with my calf muscles, and once she seemed satisfied it was indeed me in the saddle, straightened her neck to face forward again and began to walk.

"Hey, what are you doing on that horse? I'm going to take it back to the riding school!"

Natasha and Erin were closing in and coming faster towards me. They would be close enough to grab me in a few seconds more. I was going to have to try a trot. I squeezed Tiny again, and she sprang forwards into a lively bouncy trot propelling us forward and I started bouncing feeling like I was on a space hopper. I remembered the words Holly always shouted to me at this point. "Keep your heels down and rise in time with the horse."

"Slow down. I am telling. I'm gonna tell your mum and Holly and everyone so they know what you have been doing."

Natasha stopped running to rake around in her backpack for her phone. I knew I had to go faster to get away from them.

"Oh Tiny, I haven't done much cantering before, and I'm a bit scared," I said, and I grabbed a chunk of her thick, beautiful mane.

Tiny sprang on faster, and I felt the power of her canter for the first time. All this time I had been scared of cantering and here was clever little Tiny, or big Tiny should I say, showing me that it was actually easier to sit than a bouncy up and down trot.

Tiny sped along the grassy pathways, putting a bigger and bigger distance between Erin and Natasha and me, and while I was sure that they were still shouting at me from wherever they were, I couldn't hear them anymore and I'm sure they couldn't have seen me. The grass bushes sped by me, and we passed all the usual rocks, benches, and clumps of grass I often daundered past in a fraction of our usual time.

I rode along the paths that I always walked on foot to Uncle Joe's, as I sat and held Tiny's mane as we rocked and swayed along the paths. We were out of sight of Natasha and Erin by now. My hair was pushing backwards in the wind to match Tiny's.

"Okay, Tiny, I need to slow you down and make you small again so I can carry you over the stream," I told her. "I usually have to leap on the stepping-stone halfway and do it in two jumps so you will need to be little."

Tiny had other ideas and as I faffed about trying to shorten my reins into a good grip to slow her down, she arrived at the stream. "Oh, Tiny, I don't know how to do this...I haven't had any jumping! Oh, right...well, I have now, then!" I told her as she landed on the other end of the stream and slowed back down to a trot, and then to a walk. I held her mane with one hand and stroked her neck with the other gloating to myself. My first jump and Tiny has taught me how. I was buzzing with the knowledge I had just jumped the stream, I never thought I would have managed to stay on. Exhilaration pumped through me. I just had one little problem. I wasn't quite sure how to get back off Tiny. The ground looked so far away.

Fifteen

Chapter 15

I could see the entranceway to Uncle Joe's driveway, and he had left the workshop door open. I rode Tiny into the workshop and stood her next to the big table to climb down. First, I climbed off Tiny and onto the table, and then, keeping a hold of her reins, I climbed off the table onto the ground.

"Stay still and don't knock anything over," I told Tiny as I pulled my backpack off and raked around in my bag for the machine.

"We have to be quick, Tiny. What if Uncle Joe comes and finds a pony in his workshop? It might be hard to explain."

I pulled the machine out and pointed it at Tiny as I snatched my glasses from my face. Without wearing my glasses, I couldn't see who was treading on the gravel up the driveway towards us as it crunched under their feet. I steeled my nerves to stop myself from snatching my glasses back on to steal a glance at who it was. I had to try and be fast, and get Tiny shrunk back down to a hideable size before they got here. I flicked the on/off button and pressed the switch.

"Woof-Woof!" Phew! It had only been Bessie on the gravel. I breathed a sigh of relief as I heard the familiar *Whirr-Whirr-Whirr*—and suddenly Tiny was huge. Her ears were popping up to the roof of the big shed.

"Oh, what have I done? You're taking up the whole shed; how come you're so massive?" I was now only up to Tiny's knees and she lowered her head to sniff me.

I looked at the machine and saw that in my rush, I'd put my glasses the maximising way round. I quickly turned them around and tried to encourage Tiny to stay still. She scratched her bum with her teeth and her turning her head lifted me off my feet as I hung on to the reins.

"Come on, Tiny, work with me here." I ran back round to the machine and pressed the button...*whir whirr whirr zoomp.*

"Thank goodness, you're normal-sized again, Tiny. I'm not sure I could have found enough food for you at that size," I said. "Now stay still one sec." I pressed the button again, and Tiny was her perfect Tiny pocket size again.

Bessie was barking like mad. "Get off Bessie, get away from Tiny," I told her as I plucked her off the ground and into the safety of my lunchbox. I could hear crunching on the gravel as I popped my lunchbox back into my backpack and Uncle Joe appeared in the doorway. "Oh, it's you, Lilly, I wondered what all the barking was for. I thought you'd have been straight in the house for your yard show tonight and your normal snack. Anyway, I think there's a burger van there tonight. An old school friend popped in today to ask me to fix her hair straighteners and she seemed to know all about it."

"Oh, great Uncle Joe, I'm ready when you are. I can't wait."

"Why are all the tools on the floor? What's happened here?"

I saw Uncle Joe's spanner collection had been strewn all over the floor from the shelf where it sat, and his socket set was lying in pieces everywhere. "Oh, I'm so sorry, I had a little fall."

"How could you fall and knock down all these tools when they were at opposite sides? Are you okay?" He didn't sound angry, just concerned.

"I'm sorry Uncle Joe, I'll get them." I started putting them all back in their specific places. I knew it was really important to Joe, that all the tools went right into the correct spaces all organised for when he goes to do his next project.

"I'll help you; we don't want to be late. I'm quite looking forward to it, now I know my old school friend is going to be there."

"That's great, Uncle Joe. How come you don't see them more often?"

"Well, we did, but then when her career took off, she moved into the city. That's where all the high-flying jobs are, I suppose. We lost touch."

Sixteen

Chapter 16

The riding school had set a wonderful course of jumps up in the arena. They were playing their jumping night music over the tannoys and the seating stand was full of people eating tasty burgers from the van that filled the air with the smell of ketchup, grease, and onions.

"Uncle Joe, can we go and watch the warm-up ring?" I asked. Some of the ponies had started coming in.

"Sure. I might go say hello to Holly. I think she wanted me to take a look at her clippers. I'll meet you back at the main arena seating in half an hour?"

"Yeah, great." I stood and watched the ponies coming into the ring.

Little Robin was on Smartie; how cute. I saw her mum standing near me.

"Robin is doing the show tonight? That's amazing," I said.

Robin's mum moved her eyes off her phone screen and looked at me.

"Oh yeah, you're the girl who leads her in her lessons. Milly, is it? Yeah, we have a helper leading her tonight as well. She's going to do the lead rein classes—" and before I could wish her good luck or ask more questions her eyes were locked back into her phone screen.

I went for a walk around the riding school barns, to see if I could see any of the horses and let little Tiny have a sniff. I saw Natasha take one of the riding school ponies out of the stables, so I went in the opposite direction. I bumped straight into Kalila.

"Oh, hi Lilly, you made it," she said, and she smiled at me. "I'm so glad to have a friend here tonight."

"You don't get nervous at shows, do you? I couldn't imagine you ever getting nervous."

"No, I just don't know anyone here. Wanna come and help me get Chintzy ready?"

"Love to; I have a bit of time before I need to go round and meet Uncle Joe."

"Did your mum say it's okay for Sunday then, to come to the big show in the lorry with me and my mum?" she asked me as we walked around to Chintzy's stable.

"I want to come but you know how parents can be with the whole stranger danger thing. I can't even phone people and get them to speak to their mums because I'm not allowed a phone yet, even though everyone else has a phone in my class."

"Oh, that's a shame. Is your mum coming later? Maybe she could meet my mum then?"

"No, I'm here with my uncle, and she would probably want to meet your mum for herself if I'm going away for the day with you both."

"That's mums though—they worry about everything. If she met my mum, she would probably just be worried that she would feed you to death. She has this thing. Like an offering everyone food all the time thing."

"Really? My mum is pretty into healthy eating stuff. Does she try to get you to eat veg all the time?"

"Only if you're Chintzy. Wait till you meet her—and don't ever tell her you're hungry or she will have a three-course meal coming out of her back pocket." Kalila laughed.

"Your saddle is so lovely," I told her as I saw it sitting over the saddle door.

"Yeah, I took it home to give it a good clean for the big show on Sunday."

I helped Kalila brush and sparkle Chintzy to perfection. I kept my backpack on and let Chintzy sniff away.

When little Tiny started whinnying to her, Chintzy took a big intake of breath and did a huge whinny back.

"Hey Chintzy, what's up with you? Are you calling to a pony that's way off in the distance? Are there ponies still out there in the fields you can hear?" Kalila asked.

I felt bad. I knew Tiny only wanted to play but she was going to get us caught.

"I'd best go back around and meet Uncle Joe. He will be worried. I'll watch you from the stadium and cheer you on for your class."

"Okay, cool, if I wave you down, will you come and grab my pony for me if I need to go for a pee or anything?"

"Yeah, sure thing. I'll be watching the whole time. I would love to hold Chintzy and get a pony cuddle halfway through."

What was it with my friends and pee incidents today?

"Fab. Take my phone, will you, and get a video of me when I'm doing my class?" Kalila offered her mobile with an outstretched arm.

I smiled and nodded as I took the phone. I loved having my own horse friend and I loved having my own pony. I just wished that they knew about each other. How nice it would be if Chintzy and Tiny could play together and hang out together as Kalila and I did.

I made my way back to the main arena and scanned the area to see if I could see Uncle Joe in the seats. I spotted him sitting front centre, watching the first of the riders in the ring. He watched little Robin being led around over some poles on the ground in a walk. I made my way over to Uncle Joe and sat beside him.

"Hey, did you find your friend?"

"Yeah, she insisted we all needed burgers so she's away to the van. How cute is that little kid on the little pony?" he asked me, looking at Robin.

"Yeah, she's adorable," I told him as I watched Robin beam with pride as her pony was led stretching its little legs over the poles with Robin's grin warming my heart.

Robin called out and waved her hands.

"Mummy, Mummy, I'm doing it. Look at me!"

She was trying to get her mum's attention. I followed Robin's gaze and saw her mum still looking at her phone screen.

"Yeah yeah, that's great, well done," she told Robin without even looking up from whoever she was texting.

A woman looked at Uncle Joe as she strolled towards him. Her long floaty dress didn't affect her ability to nimbly manoeuvre herself up the seats carrying arms full of burgers. Her hair fell over the front of her face as she looked down at the ground to pick her footing. That had to be Uncle Joe's friend. When she looked up the woman smiled at me, and I knew I had seen that face before. Of course, Kalila's mum. She carried an oversized handbag, with the grey leather straining under the weight of whatever she had crammed it full of.

"Hey, I didn't know how hungry you are, so I got you two burgers just in case!" she said, thrusting two burgers wrapped in napkins in my direction.

"Yeah, thanks," I said, wondering what to do. I obviously wanted the tasty burgers, but then I never know what to say or how to say it. I followed Uncle Joe's lead as he took a couple of burgers and bit into one.

Lubna smiled at me "I didn't realise that you were *that* Lilly. Kalila's Lilly from the stables." and I smiled back wondering what to say back before Uncle Joe saved the silence.

"Don't worry about the food thing, Lilly, she used to feed us all in our Uni days too. And she will have everything from hairbrushes to spare little ponies in that huge handbag of hers."

Lubna smiled and laughed good-naturedly as I panicked as I thought about little ponies in bags and pulled my backpack closer into my lap. I watched Uncle Joe chat away and watched the comfortableness between them as they chatted and giggled. I sat quietly munching my burger and dropping the grease down my shirt as I saw the laughs pass between them and in-jokes that could only come from years of friendship. It was nice for Uncle Joe to have a new friend, or an old friend as the case may be, to be around to hang out with him.

I turned from watching them chat, to seeing Robin was finished and leaving the arena. I saw Kalila coming and sitting astride Chintzy, looking all glamour and beauty on her elegant pony as they entered the arena. I saw sets of eyes all turning to see who this new girl to the area was on the pretty-faced pony they hadn't seen before. I left my seat, smiling at Uncle Joe and Lubna, telling them, "I'll be right back." I stood and lifted my bag and Uncle Joe looked up and called out "Hey, just leave that heavy bag on your seat and we can watch it for you." I reluctantly lowered my bag back down, not wanting to look suspicious and hoping it would be ok with Lubna and Uncle Joe there.

There were blue seats in the stadium on either side of the aisles. Watching so not to fall down the steep steps, I made my way to see Kalila.

"Hey Lilly, I'm glad you're here, can you pass my whip up? I dropped it by accident on the ground here." Kalila said.

"Sure," I said as I entered the warm-up ring and passed it up to her.

"Awesome, I'm gonna do the next class once they get the jumps put up a bit. See, they're in the main ring raising the heights now for the class before me."

I looked in the ring and saw the jumps being put up, so they were little cross poles a few inches high. Natasha and Erin saw the jumps being put up and rode their ponies across to where the warm-up ring opened up to the entrance to the main arena.

"Why are you in this arena, Lilly? You don't even have a pony hired so you shouldn't be in the warm-up ring," Natasha scolded. "We don't trust you round here with you being a pony stealer."

"I'd better go back and watch you from the stands," I told Kalila. "Is there anything you need before I go?"

"No, I could do with a can of juice, but I've lost my mum for now," Kalila answered.

"She's up chatting with my Uncle Joe. I'll try and bring a can down to you. Can you drink when you're still up there on Chintzy?"

"Hell yeah, I could live on Chintzy if I thought I would get away with it."

"Okay, I'll see what I can do," I said as Kalila started to warm her pony up in the ring by trotting around.

"Hurry up and get out of here, you're distracting me, and I will tell," Natasha told me in her smuggest voice. "You can't be here just 'cos your friend has a pony, you need to hire one of your own, you know."

Erin chimed in, "She wouldn't be allowed anyway. She can't even canter yet properly, and she hasn't had a proper jumping lesson either, like us. You're still in the little kid riding class. That's how when I told my mum about that trick that you played earlier, I realised it couldn't have been you. You will have a big cousin or something that looks like you. Who would believe that Speccy Lilly would have her own horse and be able to ride it?"

This was one of the times I wanted something smart and clever to say back, but instead, I turned and saw Kalila couldn't hear them, being at the other end of the warm-up ring. Kalila was more focused on riding her pony around in perfect circles and warming Chintzy up than chatting with Natasha and Erin. The relief that she couldn't hear the embarrassing things Natasha and Erin could say about me was comforting, but she would have known what to say if they spoke to her like that. I looked down at my shoes and tottered back to where Uncle Joe sat in the rows of seating in the stand.

"Hey Lilly, you're back. Is that your school friend just gone in the ring?" Uncle Joe asked.

"Yeah, well she's in the same class as me at school anyway," I told him.

Natasha had a great big smile on her face as she went into the ring to start her course. I heard the bell go and Lubna said, "Oh look, there's one of the riding school girls. I hope she does well. My daughter won't be in until later on."

I watched Natasha ride her pony up to the first jump and over it popped. I thought one day it would be my turn: mine and Tiny's. I checked in my bag and stroked Tiny in her lunchbox at the bottom of my bag as I watched. Natasha forgot what the next jump was, and Holly came into the ring and pointed to the number two jump. "On you go, Natasha, ride her forwards." Holly encouraged her.

I was quite far away but riding instructors always have outdoor voices, even indoors. A voice that travels made me wonder if Holly could ever whisper a secret, without letting the whole place know about it. Not that Holly needed to keep secrets. She could probably do whatever she liked and have as many ponies as she wanted. I had to admit Natasha was doing genuinely well. That is until jump number five. I saw her come tumbling off the side of her pony as she tried to land after the jump. She landed on the floor and her pony went for a canter alone around the arena.

Holly chased the pony until she caught her by the reins and brought her back to Natasha, who was still picking herself back up off the floor. "Never mind, Natasha, just pop back on and give it another go. In this class, it's just for fun so you can do one more jump to get your confidence back before you leave the arena."

"I don't want to. You gave me a stupid pony. It made me fall," Natasha told her.

"It's all part of learning. Now, on you get, and straight over that jump there."

Holly coaxed Natasha and gave her a leggy back on. Natasha kicked the pony hard over the jump...too hard and after it popped over and landed on the other side it didn't want to stop. They sped off, unexpectedly, belting around the outside track of the arena.

"Sit up and pull the reins, Natasha," I heard Holly shout.

Natasha looked so terrified. It was hard not to smirk even a little, so I focused on Tiny in the bottom of my bag. I was feeding her little bits of hay Rebecca had given me at school earlier. Tiny seemed so chilled; just loving the smell and sound of being at a riding school seemed to calm her, bringing her a familiarity that she must have been craving.

Lots of riders went in one by one after Natasha had finished and tried their luck around the course. I looked up and saw Holly coming toward us. I dreamed of my ideal scenarios in my head and hoped maybe I was going to be allowed to have a little shot of one of the ponies, but it was far more likely that she was going to ask me to help put the jumps up for the next class.

Holly smiled at me as she walked up to me, then passed me, and turned to Lubna who was still chatting to Uncle Joe.

Holly said to her, "Kalila and Chintzy seem to have settled in well. She's signed up for the bigger classes. Just checking if that's okay as she hasn't been here long enough for me to know where she is at with her riding."

Lubna stopped chatting with Joe and smiled at Holly. "Oh, I must thank you for looking after them both since they have arrived here. Yeah, just let her do what classes she fancies, she will be fine. Just a practice run for her when she goes to the Pony Championships at the weekend."

"No worries. She seems to be well bonded with her pony. They're in the warm-up ring and I know she's on full livery, but she loves doing most things for her pony herself," Holly said.

"Yeah, that's my Kalila. She would have Chintzy sleeping in her bed at home if I let her."

The adults laughed that way, which lets you know that they are all relaxed with each other.

"Here Holly, it must be hungry work running around with all the riders you have jumping, take a chocolate bar," Lubna said, passing her a bar covered in shiny purple paper.

I suddenly realised as the adults chatted that if they all knew each other then maybe that would change things about me going to the show! I had to tell Uncle Joe it was Lubna I was going with so maybe I would be allowed to go with them on the weekend. I best go and let Kalila know as she would know what to say to the adults, I just get the nerve up to ask for a drink to take down to Kalila first.

Lubna interrupted my thoughts and said, "Lilly, if you are going back down to stand by the warm-up ring barriers can you take Kalila a can of juice, please? She always gets a thirst before these things. And take some sweets for her just in case," she said as she piled my hands full of chocolate bars. Problem solved. Maybe it was the night for solving problems if I could just speak up, maybe give it a try. I peered over at Uncle Joe.

"Kalila's the girl I told you about Uncle Joe, my new friend who said I could go to the show with her at the weekend," I explained.

"Oh right, well I'm sure your mum will be fine with you going if it's with Lubna," Uncle Joe looked at Lubna and said, "I think you might pass her not a serial killer test since you partied together at university."

Lubna said, "You'd be most welcome, and I've already been instructed by Kalila I'm not allowed to do my crazy singing in the horse lorry this weekend as we have a friend coming."

First Tiny, now being allowed to go to the show, and of course getting to watch Natasha fall off. Could this day get any better?

Seventeen

Chapter 17

"Watch my bag Uncle Joe," I asked as he chatted to Lubna and I sped down to deliver the juice, sweets and good news to Kalila. She saw me standing with the juice by the barriers to the warm-up ring and she said, "Thanks Lilly, you brought me the juice, *and* a tonne of sweets, which suggests you found my mum."

"Yeah, it turns out she used to hang out with my mum in University days and is a friend of my uncle's so I'm probably going to be allowed to come at the weekend after all."

"That's amazing. I'm so pleased. It's defo more fun going with a friend."

"Yeah, I noticed that. I think Uncle Joe is enjoying that trait right now. He's at least two burgers in."

"Look, that's my class starting, all the jumps are up. I can't wait. I love this bit."

"Aren't you scared when they are all so high?"

"Not on Chintzy. I just need to hold on to his mane and hope for the best. He's a sweet little pony."

They rode out of the warm-up ring and into the main arena to do their class and I stood by the barrier so I could get a better view.

Kalila circled the pony in a nice bouncy canter as though it was the easiest thing in the world and a bell went off. She looked straight at the jump and rode forward towards it into a bigger canter. The jump seemed huge, and I shut my eyes as Chintzy and Kalila approached the brightly coloured poles on big jump stands. When I opened my eyes again, they were over the first jump and heading for the next one. I could just about trust she would go over them safely now. I clapped as she landed and watched Chintzy and Kalila soar over the jumps as if they were born to fly over them.

"Come on, come on," I willed her. I realised I was more excited than she was.

As she finished her course my eyes were wide. One day that would be me and Tiny! I wished anyway. Kalila rode into the warm-up ring on Chintzy. I ran over the barrier on that side of the arena and called out, "You did it, you did it."

"Not yet I haven't. If I go clear, I get a timed round with the others who went clear."

"What's clear?"

"It means we didn't knock any down or anything. It's just practice anyway; it's fine either way. But thanks for the encouragement. I think my mum is all ponied out. She isn't even watching now."

I looked over and Lubna and Uncle Joe were gone, and more importantly, so was my bag with Tiny.

I turned and ran around the arena hunting high and low for them. I checked the snack bar. Toilets! Whenever you can't find a grown-up, they are always in the toilets. I dashed there.

OMG, what if Uncle Joe hasn't picked up my bag, or what if he looks in it or puts all Lubna's cans of juice in and crushes little Tiny! What am I going to do?

My heart thudded in my chest as I tried to figure out what to do. Poor Tiny was so reliant on me and now I had lost her.

I ran out to the car park to see if Uncle Joe's car was still there; surely, he wouldn't leave without me. I saw the car but no Uncle Joe.

What if he had thrown Tiny into the cold dark boot, or Natasha had taken my bag?

Then I saw Lubna standing by her horse lorry saying, "Yeah, just like you to have a spare bulb to fit my horse lorry. You always were a boy scout," and up stood Uncle Joe from behind the horse lorry bonnet.

I went running over as fast as my legs could carry me. "Uncle Joe, where's my bag?"

"Your bag?"

"Yeah, my backpack. Where is it?"

"I don't know."

My heart stopped thudding and felt as if it had stopped forever. I started to feel sick.

"Oh, I have it dear, I picked it up and brought it with us; are you looking for a snack in it? I have some crisps here if you want them," said Lubna.

"Where did you put the bag?" I gasped.

"I put it with our bags to keep it safe, dear. Go into the front passenger side of the lorry. They are all there."

I ran round to the lorry door and was surprised with the height I had to leap to get in. I saw the bag on the passenger seat, upright and all safe and sound and felt relief fill my body.

I grabbed my bag and lifted it up. It was all soggy on the bottom. Gooey yuck covered the bottom of my bag. I was scared to look inside. What if poor Tiny had been splattered and all little Tiny bits were running out?

I opened the backpack and saw little Tiny eating grass and munching calmly in her little lunch box.

Lubna looked over and saw the sogginess at the bottom of my bag. "Oh sorry, sweetie, I might have put the bag on the eggs. I collected them from the chickens at the house before I came over, and I meant to bring some to give to Holly."

I smiled. "It's no problem."

As long as it's not Tiny guts splattered everywhere it's no problem at all, I thought. I kept the opening to my bag small enough that I could peek in but anyone else further away couldn't so I could watch in private. How sweet little Tiny was.

I put my hand underneath and saw the letter from Mrs Zanya was all eggy and yuck. Well, there was another reason not to give it to my mum. If I was in detention until she got the letter to come up and see Mrs Zanya, maybe I would rather just stay in detention forever. The letter being all eggy now was like a sign. There was no way I would be able to do the weekend show if my mum knew I was in bother at school.

I looked up from watching Tiny to tell Lubna, "Kalila went clear in her class."

"Oh, that's nice, sweetie. I always tell her it doesn't matter if you knock them all down. It's whether you and your pony have fun that counts."

I thought that's the way Tiny and I would look at it if we ever had the chance.

I loved sitting with Uncle Joe and Lubna watching Kalila do her jump-off in her class. The night drew on as all the riders in their shiny hats, all with lovely smart jodhpurs and much-loved ponies, gave it their best efforts. Fat ponies, large horses, small ponies, ponies with long manes and ponies with plaits, but none as lovely as my precious Tiny. Watching Kalila get her pretty rosette before Uncle Joe took me home was the icing on the cake.

"Okay, dear, I'll phone your mum and make sure she is okay with you coming with me, Joe says she's never changed her number, so I'll buzz her in the morning," Lubna said.

"Thanks," I told her as I was leaving. What an amazing night—spending all that pony time and still having more to look forward to. And better still I could have loads of pony time from the joy of my house when I got home.

I popped into Uncle Joe's car, pulled my seatbelt on and wrapped my arms around my backpack holding it on my lap. "I can't believe that you know her from years back. I've been desperate to go to the show."

"I'm sure your mum will be fine now it turns out we all know each other. I bet you're pleased."

"I am over the moon. I have never got to go to a proper big horse show before. I don't even know what classes there are."

"Take my phone out of the glove compartment and look it up, though it seems to me that your friend will be mostly into the jumping classes."

Uncle Joe's phone told me that the jumping classes were to be in the main arena starting from 8 am and go on most of the day. There was a ring 1 for dressage and a ring 2 for showing classes. Other arenas were assigned for the jumping classes which were divided into heights. The dressage into different numbers didn't make much sense to me. A certain class caught my eye when I saw the showing section had a native cob class with *Entries on the day*. If only, I thought. I pictured in my head what would happen if I took Tiny out of my backpack and put her on the judges' table. I wondered if hamster-sized ponies were allowed.

Uncle Joe interrupted my daydream with, "I'll just pop in with you and speak to your mum about the show at the weekend. She will be pleased to hear her old friend's back in town."

I ran through the front door with my backpack in my hand, excited to hear my mum let me know it was okay.

"Hey Julie, you will never guess who I bumped into at the..." Uncle Joe's words trailed off as he laid eyes on my mum, sitting looking at the laptop at the dining room table with tears running down her face. My mum always knew what to do, so if she was crying, something had to be wrong big time.

Eighteen

Chapter 18

What if she was sick? Or someone had died.

"Lilly, go up to your room till I chat with your mum."

I ignored Uncle Joe and went over to my mum and put my arms around her. Mum smiled through her teary face and said, "Sorry pet, it's okay."

Joe pulled up a chair at the table and sat opposite Mum. "What's wrong? What is it?"

"I've lost my job today." Mum whispered.

Guilt rushed over me as I remembered how misplacing Tiny this morning had made her late. I decided that Mum's tears were all my fault and if I had just kept a hold of Tiny better, be more responsible like Mum's always saying, she would still have her job. My heart lurched as I absorbed that I was the cause of all Mum's tears. She had warned me that this would happen if I made her late.

"What happened?" Uncle Joe asked her as I popped the kettle on to make everyone tea. It's such a British thing. When you don't know what to do, you make everyone a cup of tea, and of course with chocolate for good measure. I looked at Mum's face and saw healthy eating wasn't going to be her priority tonight, so I climbed up to her secret chocolate stash. The stash wasn't a well-kept secret since we were the only two people who lived here and we both knew where it was.

Uncle Joe always took my side and fought my corner but as mum sniffed and snuffled back her crying so she could reply I knew that causing my Mum this upset would make him disappointed in me.

"They said they are making me redundant, but I don't think they've liked me for a while. I wanted to develop new ideas on cutting down the amount that came into the recycling plant that went to the landfill. My ideas were all going to cost them a little more but be so much better for the environment."

"So, can't you go back and ask to be kept on if you back down on the ideas?"

"No, they hate new ideas, and they have made their minds up now in any case. They said it's redundancy anyway, and you know how many jobs there are for people in recycling around here. It's that one plant or nothing."

"You could retrain, or go back to office work."

"That will all take time, and it takes so long for jobs to come up around here. I'm so worried about how to keep a roof over our heads and a car on the road."

I understood my riding lessons would currently not be a priority. I hated watching Mum feeling so sad and that gut-wrenching feeling of not being able to help her meant I didn't feel any better even after hearing that it wasn't all my fault after all.

Uncle Joe stayed late into the night reassuring my mum, listening to her and just being there. He just gets things sometimes, like situations and feelings. He went through the whole losing his job thing when he first became unwell and could only work sometimes. His good days and bad days and not knowing when would be good or bad meant he got frustrated at not being able to keep his job. He was miserable going through all of that and finally having no more to do with his old job made him seem so much happier. I just didn't feel losing her job would have that result with Mum though.

"Sorry Lilly, I'd better get you fed," Mum said to me after a while.

"I'm full. I've been eating all night," I told her.

"Oh yeah, that reminds me. Guess who her new friend at the riding school's mum is?" asked Uncle Joe.

"I don't know."

"Lubna, from university."

"No way! Has she moved back? She must come around! It will be so good to see her again." Mum sounded quite pleased, well, under the circumstances anyway.

"Does that mean that I can go to the show with her mum?" I felt guilty for asking right now but I was so desperate to go.

"Yeah, of course, Lilly, you'll be fine with her." Mum turned to Uncle Joe. "Joe, do you remember that time that you and she dressed up for that party as a submarine?"

"We were not a submarine! We were a baguette!" he corrected, and we all began to laugh. Mum looked weird laughing with tears still on her face she hadn't quite wiped away yet.

"I want to see the photos of that," I told them both.

"Yeah, no chance, it was before photos were on phones everywhere, so if I find them, they will be the old, printed copies and I will burn them before you can blackmail us forever with them."

Uncle Joe had a great habit of changing the mood like that. I was so glad he had come into the house when he dropped me off tonight. Mum's eyes were still red from crying but at least she was laughing now as she and Joe went down a path of reminiscing on old times.

I didn't have the answers to Mum's problems, and I knew she was still really sad, so I gave her some peace and went off to my room. I was glad I had little Tiny to snuggle up to in bed. She curled and snuggled in beside me and let me stroke away.

"I have learnt my lesson to always make sure and put you back in your cage at night after the fright of this morning," I told her as she looked up at me with no idea of the mayhem she had caused.

One of the things I loved about her being so small was she could come everywhere with me. She loved grazing in her cage where I had brought some turf from outside in and made a little floor of grass for her. She would nibble on the hay from Rebecca and for once there was someone who loved Mum's obsession with buying carrot sticks. I loved to groom Tiny all shiny and immaculate, and she loved being groomed so we were quite the team. She seemed used to coming around in my pocket already, so this was all working out. It was great having a new best friend that could actually live in my pocket now that Rebecca was leaving.

I wished I could share my happiness with Mum as she moped about the place looking so sad and worrying about bills and work. Everything just seemed better with a pony in my life. Maybe it would be the same for her, then again, probably not.

It took quite a few baths to get Tiny's mane and tail to perfection after her living in such a muddy field, and it was quite a surprise to find that once all the mud was washed out, she had a mane and tail that flowed like nothing on earth. I'd thought I had her clean last night, but the extra bath massively brought out all the pretty.

I remember the first time I read in my pony magazine about a horse having feathers, how ridiculous it sounded. As if ponies had feather wings and could fly away, but if ponies can be pocket-sized why not I supposed. I knew now it was the hairy bits over their feet and Tiny had beautiful ones I could brush out and admire. She had long thick hair all around her feet almost like little pony leg warmers.

I tried to get up before Mum and clean out Tiny's cage, putting fresh hay and water in, flushing her poop down the toilet and hanging out together. Our early morning was great, even though Mum was pretty sad. She seemed worried and went from saying, "Oh, I'm sorry I have let you down Lilly," to, "Those pigs at the plant. I'm gonna get something better and show them," but the worry hung over us.

Sunday just couldn't come fast enough. When it came round, I jumped out of my bed and got myself ready at ultra-fast speed.

"It's going to be cold, Lilly, get your warmest jacket on if you're going to be standing about all day."

Mum went to make me a packed lunch and I said, "It's okay, Kalila's mum said she would have loads of packed lunch."

Mum smiled and said, "She still does that? Come on then, we'd best get you there so you're not late."

I could hardly contain my excitement and wondered how Chintzy would be groomed, and if Kalila would give me more hay for Tiny. I wondered if I could watch her classes and get Tiny to have a sniff with Chintzy for some pony company.

Mum started to reverse out the drive then, *crunch*. The car came to a standstill.

"What's wrong?" I looked behind us, but we hadn't hit anything.

"Oh no, the clutch is gone. They're a fortune to fix and without a job, I can't see how I'm gonna fix it."

"Can Uncle Joe have a try?"

"He would need special tools. It's really hard to get to the clutch and he won't be able to fix it in time to get you to the riding school."

"But Mum, I've been so excited for ages, so please, can I walk or get the bus?"

"Go inside and let me try and think, okay. Be quiet just now."

My heart sank with disappointment as I knew I wasn't going to be able to get there myself.

Mum tried phoning Uncle Joe and he answered but said, "Sorry, but I've already left for today. I'm away out with my friends and I think even if I turned around I wouldn't be back for a while. I don't think I can come to get her. Why don't you try Lubna?"

Mum said, "I think the last thing she will want is detours on a morning where she has to get to a show in a hurry. I'll give her a call and let her know not to wait for you, Lilly."

My chances of going to the horse show were over. I went up the stairs and tried not to cry as I petted Tiny in my room. "I'm sorry, Tiny. It was going to be the best day ever." I stroked her mane and felt so glad I at least had my little pony for company. I just didn't know what I was going to do now I couldn't get any fresh hay for her from Kalila.

Half an hour later, a big tooting noise came from outside, so much louder than a car horn. Tiny, who was by now used to coming in cars, a day at school, and even a trip around the supermarket, jumped at the big noise. I picked her up and told her, "Don't worry Tiny, just a noise outside. Nothing to worry about."

It tooted again and I looked out my window and saw Kalila's horse lorry.

"Mum, Kalila's outside, I'm going, I'm going!" I called to her as I gathered my things into my backpack and ran towards the door.

"Oh good. She said she would try to come and get you, but I was scared to tell you in case she didn't make it and you were disappointed again."

"Bye, Mum."

"Bye, Lilly, have fun. here, take this," she said, handing me some money. "In case you need anything."

"Oh Mum, you're so worried about money just now."

"Yeah, well it's something you always wanted to do so I want it to be special for you. Don't worry about it and have a great time."

Mum stood outside and waved the lorry off as I sat in the front beside Kalila. I grinned excitedly. The loud honk of the lorry and noisy engine had the neighbours looking out their windows wondering who had brought a horse lorry into our quiet little street. Kalila pressed the radio on. She pulled her phone out of her pocket and said, "Wait, I'll put on my special playlist for going to shows."

The horse-related songs came on and we all sang along, laughing...well I joined in on the ones I knew the words to.

It was a happy little journey, with Tiny in my pocket and Chintzy in the back of the lorry, and us three singing and munching all the snacks and treats in the front. One of Kalila's favourite songs came on and she turned the volume up, bouncing on her seat and singing at the top of her voice. Lubna laughed and joined in until the end of the song when she put the volume back to where it started so we could all chat again without shouting.

"Kalila, what type of nuts are pony nuts from?" I asked.

Lubna and Kalila laughed.

"They are like just horse feed pellets, there are no nuts in them, but I can see why you think that."

"Why are they called nuts then? Can all ponies eat them?"

"Look, I've got a sack of them under my seat. Take a handful. See? They are just pellets, dead straight forward and horses love them. That's why I have them in the lorry to tempt the horses to load when they are going up the ramp."

"Oh." I joined their laughter and she put a handful from her sack into my hand. "Dare you to taste one and take a bite."

I took a sniff and bit one to see what it was like. It tasted like nothing I had tasted before. "Hmmm, it tastes like chicken," I said and Kalila, her mum and I laughed together.

"Put them in your pocket and you can use them as horse treats."

"Thanks," I said.

My panic at not being able to go was all forgotten by the time we arrived at the equestrian centre. Huge lorries, some carrying five or six horses, filled the car park. All the riders had lovely outfits and shiny boots.

Lubna said, "Right, you girls, go in the back of the lorry and get changed and I'll get Chintzy unloaded and groomed."

There were three compartments in the lorry. There was a cab that we sat in while we drove along. The back part had room for Chintzy and probably a couple of her friends if she felt that way and there was a third part in the middle.

Kalila opened the door to the middle part, and we climbed in. "This is the living quarters, and we keep the tack and stuff in here too. Right, I only get changed once we are here cos I always manage to get dirty before I get in the ring," she said, and she laughed.

She pulled open a drawer, took out some jodhpurs and a shirt and began to get changed.

She looked at me and said, "Hey, you're about four inches shorter than me. I have some of last year's stuff I don't fit anymore. If you want to get changed too, you can use this stuff."

She handed me a smart pair of jodhpurs and a shirt just like hers, but slightly smaller.

"Oh, that's so kind! I would love that. I can blend in with the rest of the horse girls," I said.

"Sure." She buttoned up her shirt as I was still trying to wriggle into my borrowed jodhpurs and she said, "What shoe size are you?"

"Four," I told her.

"Okay, Mum's probably cleaned them out the lorry cos I haven't been a four for a while but have a look in that cupboard behind you and see if there's a pair of boots. Never know we might get lucky," she said as she pulled her own boots on.

When I looked in the cupboard they were sitting there, all shining, all perfect, a spare size four.

I couldn't believe how much my luck had changed since Mum's clutch went.

As I remembered back to Mum's problems, I felt a twinge of guilt for having so much fun when Mum was back home trying to figure out what to do. Once I was changed, I put my warm winter jacket back on with Tiny still in my pocket and jumped back out of the lorry.

Lubna grinned at us. "Don't you two just look fab all scrubbed up. I've groomed Chintzy. Now you go and walk the course and I'll get his tack on for you. Don't want you to be late for your class. The jumping is in the main indoor ring, not the outside rings round the back."

Kalila and I walked towards a big building, and I asked her, "What does *walking the course* mean?"

"Dunno, just have a wee look at the course and the jumps and figure out how I'm gonna do it with Chintzy before I get on her, I suppose."

"This is so cool, I never actually got to be in the ring before at a competition. Are you okay?"

"I'm good, but I'm getting a little nervous now I think."

"Really? You? Nervous? But you weren't nervous on Wednesday."

"Yeah, this one's different, I suppose, as the jumps are a lot bigger, and I need to do well to qualify for another show."

She was right, the jumps were higher than Chintzy.

"I thought you were fearless. I'm sure you will do great."

"I'm glad I have someone here with me. Some of the girls that compete here can be so bitchy."

"Yeah, it can be like that at my school as well."

We walked around the arena and back to the lorry to find Chintzy all tacked up by Lubna without a hair out of place.

"Did your mum used to ride? She's good at all the horse stuff."
I asked

"Yeah, she did, she told me she used to ride with your mum,"
Kalila answered.

"My mum can ride?" I asked in surprise.

"You didn't know? She doesn't still ride? Last night, Mum
showed me an old photo of them about our age going out on a trek
on ponies together." Kalila told me.

"Oh my, I never knew. She just never mentioned it."

I suppose she's been so busy with work and trying to keep the
bills paid and stuff, I thought. I was confused that she would never
mention such a big thing.

"I think she won some pretty cool things back in the day." Kalila
told me.

"Really? Did Uncle Joe ride?" I had to ask.

"I don't know. She didn't mention that," she said as she led
Chintzy over to the mounting block and popped on.

"Can you go over to the board by the arena and see how many
names down I am? My class starts at ten, but I have no idea where I
am on the list."

I ran over and saw a whiteboard with a huge list of names.
I scanned my eyes down and saw her name on the list next to
Chintzy's.

"You're second," I told her, as she passed me.

"Right, can you tell my mum I need to go warm up if I am
second up?"

"Your mum watches this one?"

"Yeah, this show's a much bigger deal for us."

I ran and found Lubna in the seating stands surrounding the
arena. She sat with her big picnic basket, laughing with some other
pony mums and had my bag with her.

"Hi, I was to tell you that Kalila is second, and she is warming up," I told her.

"Oh, great dear, I brought your bag. Are you going to watch it with me?" Lubna asked.

"Yeah, can't wait." The lights, the buzzers, the announcements on the tannoy and the playing music through the arena made the atmosphere truly exciting. I felt in my pocket and checked that Tiny was still okay.

"*Neiiighhhh*!" she said excitedly. I panicked and turned around to see who had heard the neighing from my pocket. They were all busy watching the horses and with all the snorts, cantering hoof noises and other horses whinnying nobody noticed a thing. Or if anyone did, they thought it was a big neigh far off in the distance rather than a little neigh from right here in my pocket.

I heard a name come over the Tannoy and Lubna nudged me. "That's Kalila's class started. That will be the girl before her going in now."

"Awesome! So, what are the rules?" I asked.

"Well, she mustn't knock any down, fall off, or have her pony run past a jump or stop at the last minute," Lubna explained.

"I don't want any of these things to happen to her," I said feeling a bit worried.

Lubna laughed. "Neither does she. I think this class is quite important to her as it qualifies her for the Royal Highland next year and it's a big deal for us."

The girl before Kalila looked as if she had been born sitting on her horse. They moved as one. I wondered if there was ever a day that she had struggled to move in time with the rising trot or was scared to canter.

She began to make her way around the course making lovely scopey jumps over each one, looking glued to the saddle. The girl had a long flowing ponytail that flicked up high as she went over each jump.

"Watch number five. That one's going to be tricky. That's when you will see a lot of ponies play up," Lubna whispered, not taking her eyes off the rider.

"Why?" I asked.

"Cos they've decorated it with big yellow plastic sunflowers. That will freak a lot of the horses out."

The girl approached jump five, and at the very last second, the horse stopped dead. The rider sat bolt upright and looked as if she was about to be unseated. She somehow managed to stay aboard and circled the horseback around and into the jump. The girl pushed the horse forward and the second time they approached the jump they flew over.

"She will have faults now you see, so she won't be able to do the jump-off and probably won't be placed."

"Oh, what if that happens to Kalila?" I asked.

"She will have noticed it when she's been walking the course. Chintzy trusts her, so let's hope it all goes well."

The first girl finished her course and the tannoy announced she had accrued three faults.

I heard Kalila's name on the tannoy and Lubna and I sat gaping at the arena as she trotted in.

I had butterflies just watching her and I was holding my breath, wanting her to get her clear just as badly as she did. A buzzer sounded, and off she went.

"See, she has a nice rhythm in her canter there, so if she can go straight over the middle of each jump like that it will help her."

I held my breath every jump and when they got to jump five, I was frozen in my seat. The bright yellow sunflowers looked as menacing as any flowers ever had. Chintzy went towards the jump and swoosh, she went right over.

I heard Lubna breathe out and realised she was just as relieved as me. We cheered and clapped. I relaxed a bit, watching Kalila finish her course.

"Why are these jumps so close together for the next two?" I asked.

"That's a double; don't worry, they are good at them."

Lubna and I were standing clapping as Kalila rode out the arena as the tannoy announced "clear round," and played a sound clip of congratulatory music.

She's in the jump-off now, which is fab. Did you notice how many other riders were in her class, dear?"

"About thirty."

"Okay. Can you take her this can of juice?"

I hurried to congratulate Kalila, can in hand. "That was amazing, well done."

"Thanks, I'm so happy I got through. Some of the riders here are great."

"You all look amazing to me," I said looking around at how incredible all the riders seemed.

"No, I stick my elbows out like a chicken over the jump. None of us can be perfect. Can you hold Chintzy until I run to the loo?" Kalila asked.

"Sure," I said, taking a hold of his reins.

I felt in my pocket and lifted Tiny out to get a better view of Chintzy. Tiny stretched her neck forward to have a sniff and let out her biggest, "*Neiiiiiiigh,*" which wasn't actually very big as a hello to Chintzy. Chintzy returned the favour by saying hello with her biggest, "*Neigh,*" which was massive.

Lubna came over and said, "I'll hold Chintzy. You go and hang with Kalila, and I'll keep him walking around."

I ran into the bathroom after Kalila. There were girls everywhere. "Kalila?" I called out.

"Yeah, come in," came a voice from up the far end of the toilets. I walked in the direction and heard her unlock the door in the rear cubicle and call out "In here, Lilly."

We truly were friends now. The kind of friends that can share a toilet cubicle. I knew I had to tell someone apart from Rebecca about Tiny; someone who knew how to look after ponies and who would make sure I was doing everything okay. I was just worried that if I told her that she wouldn't keep the secret. I was thinking about what to do when Tiny let out another big neigh, looking for Chintzy.

"Ha-ha, did someone bring a horse in the loos? Did you hear that?" Kalila asked.

"Ehhh..." I thought about if this was the right time to tell.

"Are you okay up there watching? It's not too boring for you hanging about, is it? I wish you had your own pony to ride." Kalila chattered away as she fixed her jodhpurs and flushed the loo.

"I'm loving it here," I told her.

"*Neigh*," called out Tiny again.

I hung my jacket up on the hook before I took my turn to pee. I didn't want to lose poor Tiny from her falling out of my pocket and down the loo. That's what happened to Rebecca's mobile phone last year.

"Hey, can I have a couple of these pony nuts back for a sec for giving Chintzy before I get back on?" she asked.

"Yeah, sure, just give me a minute," I said. Kalila saw my jacket hanging up and slid her hand into my pocket looking for a pony nut and, mid peeing flow, I couldn't stop her.

"Hey what's this? Feels warm for a pony nut."

"No, it's the other pocket. You're in the wrong one."

But it was too late, and she pulled Tiny out.

"Oh, this looks so real! That's amazing. Where did you get this?"

"This is Tiny. She is real."

Kalila turned Tiny upside down and looked at her tummy. "Where do the batteries go? I haven't seen one of these before."

"She's a real pony, just really small."

Kalila must have understood, then, because she turned Tiny the right way up. "Oh, she's amazing...but how? She's so lovely."

Kalila played gently with Tiny as I explained the full story.

"It's such a shame you don't have tack. If you can make her big, you could do one of the *Enter on the day* classes."

"I do have tack. It's in my bag."

"Oh my gosh, it's ages until my jump-off. Let's see if we can get Tiny in for a class."

"I can't ride that well. I don't think I would manage. I have only cantered once and that was an emergency. Come on, let's go and see Chintzy."

We ran outside. Lubna had taken Chintzy's tack off and had her settled in a day stable. "It's a while until the jump-off, so you will need to warm Chintzy up again before his class," Lubna told Kalila. "Why don't you pair go and watch some of the other competitions and I can catch up with some of the women I used to ride with?"

"Great idea, Mum," Kalila told her, closing the stable door behind us.

Lubna wandered off, leaving us two grinning at each other with our secret surprise.

"Okay, let's get her out then. What's her name?"

"Tiny. I didn't think about how big she was when she was sized back up when I named her."

We laughed and Kalila asked, "How much room do you need to make her big again?"

"Just like a normal horse-sized bit of room," I told her.

"Follow me, the stable next door is empty for now, nothing but a clean straw bed in there. So, show me how it's done."

"Make sure you're a lookout—tell me if anyone's coming, okay?"

I sat my bag down and told her everything as I pulled it out. "This is Tiny in her safe little lunchbox with breathing holes for safety when she's in my bag, this is the machine that does it, but I need to add my glasses into the lens bit first and then aim it at Tiny."

"Okay, can you remember how to get the saddle and bridle on?"

"Yeah, Holly taught me at the riding school, but maybe we should put the saddle and bridle on now while she's still small, so they all get bigger at the same time."

"Can I help?"

"Yes, please."

"I still can't believe this is real, it's like putting a saddle on a toy pony. She is so small and cute."

"I know. I love it that she's small enough to bring into my bed at night."

"Can I borrow the machine to bring Chintzy home for a night? I would love that. It's like a dream."

"Defo, I can make Chintzy small for you after the show, if you like."

"Yes! Thank you. That will be so much fun. We can let them play together in my bedroom when they are super tiny" Kalila gushed.

I loved watching my friend's gasps of amazement as I used my glasses like some kind of magic tool to work the machine, and her face as she saw Tiny zoomed up to big.

"She stays super shiny when she grows. What a beautiful pony. Chintzy is going to love her."

"I think they do like one another; they might have had a little sniff at each other when she was still small."

"Who else have you told? Who else knows?"

"We need to keep it a secret because I don't want anyone to take this away. It's like the one magic thing I always wanted and all my dreams coming true. It keeps me going when everything is going wrong around me."

"I get it, that's what Chintzy is to me, so I won't tell a soul. It is just me that knows?"

"Just you and my best friend Rebecca, well, I hope she's still my best friend. She's moving, and I might not get to see her much anymore."

"Well, we can be best friends too and then you will have at least one either way."

I looked at her and smiled. "Besties."

*Kalila led us to the big mounting block in the car park and helped me get on.

"How did you know this was even here?"

"I've been coming for ages; come on, I'll show you where the small cross pole clear rounds are, and you can have a look and see if you want to try on Tiny. I can run into the judges' office and book you in if you want and you can enter on the spot."

"That's amazing, I thought you had to qualify for the shows here."

"Yeah, some of them but not all the classes." She started to run ahead.

Tiny jumped forward as Kalila started to run and I said, "wow" and grabbed a chunk of mane to hold on to, surprised by the sudden movement. I felt a bit wary that Tiny was very excited with all the horses milling around. Kalila glanced over her shoulder backwards at me. She saw the expression on my face and came back to Tiny's shoulder and said, "Do you want me to take the reins for you until we get you round to the ring?"

"Yeah, is that allowed?"

"Defo, I can even put you on a lead rein for the class if you wanted, but you will both likely be more relaxed and your usual selves after five minutes in the warm-up ring."

I was so grateful as she held Tiny's rein and led us round towards the ring. We hadn't even got as far as the ring before Tiny and I were feeling more chilled out and Kalila had let go.

"Right," she told me, "on the left, that's the warm-up ring. You warm up with a bit of walk and trot in there, even a wee canter if you're feeling brave. There's a practice ring. On the right, you see the course. The jumps are all numbered. It's a special clear round class they have here just to give people an experience if it's their horse's first time out at a show. Or their first time. They even change the jumps down to really small if you want but they are already tiny crosses. They will even let me come in the ring while you do it if you want me to."

"Really? It's so different from your class. There's no arena seating, or tannoys, so it seems a lot less fancy."

"Yeah, we all started off somewhere. Don't worry, you can build up to it. This is fun where everyone gets a nice rosette so long as you get a clear round. Do you want to watch a couple of people before I sign you up?"

"No, I defo want to do it. I can see from the warm-up ring, but the girl in just now is just really young. Is it just for really wee kids?"

"No, look at the woman waiting to go in after her. She has a big dressage horse. It's just a good way of getting your horse out and about at shows. It's for anyone that wants to join in."

I passed Kalila the money Mum had given me to use as my entry fee. Kalila opened the gate to let me and Tiny in the ring and then she ran over to the judges' box.

I walked around the outside of the riding arena and tried to watch what the other riders were doing. They were walking and trotting around in circles and figures of eight. There was a young kid on a Shetland being led around by her mum and a huge horse cantering around the outside. I saw what Kalila meant. It indeed was for everyone. The one thing I felt we all had in common was when you passed another horse in the ring for the first time the other rider would smile and acknowledge you.

I remembered I was wearing all the correct riding gear and felt so proud up on my very own dream shiny black pony prancing around the ring feeling that at least I looked the part.

"Hey, over here," Kalila called out as she came back from the judge's box. I walked towards the barriers so we could chat over them.

"You just go in whenever you're ready. You look great up there by the way. You're a fab match." Kalila told me.

"But I don't know what to do. I haven't done a course of jumps before," I said.

"It's okay, it's not you who does the jumps. It's Tiny who will jump them. The main secret to jumping is to aim for the middle of the jump, squeeze your pony into it and hope for the best."

"That's it? It looks more difficult than that."

"Yeah, you start with that and build up from there. And anyway, I'll come in with you."

My butterflies were going off ten to the dozen. I felt all my dreams were coming true and even if I couldn't ever ride again if I could just have this one special moment with my special pony all of my own, I would be the happiest person alive.

"Okay, one more trot round and I'm ready," I told her.

She ran and opened the gate to let me in and said to the lady, "My friend's ready."

I pointed Tiny towards the gate and pushed her on. My butter-flies and joy competed to see which emotion could be the strongest, excitement or nerves.

"Okay, just circle around and trot over the first jump when you're ready. I can run next to you and Tiny in this one."

I circled Tiny and headed towards the first jump. Kalila jogged by our side keeping up with us.

"That's it, just aim straight for the middle and when you land head for jump two," Kalila said.

I grabbed a chunk of mane as we went over the jump and was glad I had as I landed wonky to one side. I got myself straight again in the saddle and Kalila pointed ahead. "Right, there's jump two, put your weight in the stirrups this time so you keep your balance as you go over the jump."

"Eh, my weight in my stirrups, what does that even mean?" I asked her but jump two was already right in front of us and Tiny was popping over it. I bounced and landed on the other side of the saddle and pushed myself upright.

"That way for jump three." She pointed at a bigger cross pole. "It means slightly to stand in the stirrups, and..." Her voice trailed off as Tiny popped over jump three. This time I tried to almost stand putting some weight onto my feet and I landed nicely and softly in the right place.

"You got it. Four's a double, just keep pointing at her in the middle of the jump and squeezing her sides all the way through it and you will be fine."

"What's a double again? Your mum said it was two in a row or something?" I asked as Tiny popped over a small jump. I then saw a jump straight after I landed marked jump four-b, and with no time to regain my balance we had to take off again. I landed and told her, "I see what she means"

"Yeah, keep going, you're doing great." Kalila was out of breath now. Running that fast to try and keep up with me was a tough call for even someone of her fitness.

I saw jump five and remembered to head straight for the middle and squeezed Tiny on and she seemed to have the hang of it far better than me by now. We popped over it and my nerves had gone and just the excitement and exhilaration of doing the jumps as a team with Tiny filled me. I landed the jump and scanned my head around to see jump six had flowerpots under it.

"It's the last one. Go you, you can do it!" Kalila called out, and we ran straight at it and over, landing nicely before trotting away.

The lady with the big basket of rosettes clapped and said, "Well done, was that your first time on this pony? Your friend said it was."

"Yeah, it's my first time ever doing a course. Oh my, that was amazing." I gushed.

"You did great, and as you didn't knock any down you and your lovely pony can have a rosette," she said, handing me a pretty pink rosette. I beamed with pride as Kalila opened the gate back to the warm-up ring and she called out, "Go you, your first rosette! That's awesome."

I felt so proud of Tiny and stroked her neck as I kept her in an active walk around the arena to cool her off. You know that feeling you get when your dreams come true? Well, when it happens there's a tingle that goes right through you and that's what I felt right then.

I managed to ride Tiny all the way back to the stable next to Chintzy without being led by the reins this time. My shoulders pushed back to make room for my heart which had swelled with pride. I jumped off and Kalila and I quickly untacked Tiny before tacking up Chintzy.

"Let's just leave her big for a bit. She won't stand out here, and she can do stable stuff while you're doing your jump-off with Chintzy," I said.

We quickly tacked up Chintzy and took her round to the ring. Lubna was sitting on the seats chatting with a group of other mums, laughing away, and having fun. I ran over to say hi and to let her know that Kalila was in the warm-up ring in plenty of time for her class.

"Oh, hi dear. That's fab, yeah, she's good at being on time for her classes, and she's just enough time to go. Can you just take her this chocolate bar and can of juice down to make sure she's okay before she goes in the ring?"

I ran back down and handed her the juice and the chocolate over the barrier of the warm-up ring. "Aren't you nervous, with all these people watching in this main ring?"

"Well, I'm nervous in case I don't get through as I have to do it against the clock for the time in this round, but I'm not worried about the actual jumping. It's just pretty much the same as what you did. Hold on, aim them at the middle, and hope for the best!" She smiled at me.

"And stand a little in the stirrups?" I asked.

She handed me the empty can of juice back and laughed. "Exactly."

I ran back up to the stands to watch once her name was called out to get a better view and this time, she was so different in the ring. Instead of slow and steady she was zoom zoom zoom.

Lubna stopped chatting with the other ladies and turned around to watch. "Yeah, come on, that's my girl!" She cheered her on.

They ran round the course so fast; I wasn't sure how she was able to sit and balance for the turns, and I held my breath. I saw she had one jump with an a, b, and c, wow a triple. She got to the end of the course and the tannoy announced fifty-four seconds.

"Did she win?" I asked Lubna.

"She won't know until all the riders who got through to the jump off have their times. She did well, though."

I ran back down to watch her cool off in the warm-up ring and walked back round to Chintzy's stable with her. I stroked Tiny's head as I passed the stable she was in, and then I helped Kalila untack.

We both brushed down our ponies, shouting through the stable door to each other. It was amazing to be able to brush down Tiny in a proper stable when she was full size like all the other horses. This is bliss, I thought. This must be what it's like to have my own pony in a stable just next door...even if it's just for a day.

"Hey, it's a shame we can't do this all the time with shows and grooming next door to each other. I like to spend ages just brushing and plaiting Chintzy here." Kalila said.

"Same, it's just amazing isn't it, being able to properly cuddle into Tiny's neck and bury my face in her mane," I said.

"There's nothing better than pony cuddles, especially when it's your own pony."

"Too right! Oops, I need to pee again with all that juice your mum keeps giving us. I'll just make Tiny small again before I go, and I can bring her with us."

"Okay, wait for me. I wanna watch it. I've never seen a pony made small before."

I pulled the machine out of my backpack as Kalila came in and I flicked on the switch. I put my glasses into position and pressed the button. *Whir-whir-whir!*

Tiny once again became tiny, and I popped her in her little box in my backpack for the way home. Kalila led Chintzy round to her horse lorry to load it inside. As Lubna faffed about for the keys to the lorry to get the ramp down my eyes wandered around me to see who was yelling. I could hear a woman shouting from somewhere in the distance like she was having a really bad day. Then a woman with a small child caught my eye. She was holding a little pony, her hair looking like she had been rolling in the muck heap. A small pony with a matching red headcollar and lead rope set dragged the lady away from the ramp to their big blue horse trailer. She dragged the woman in the opposite direction from where she wanted to go as though she weighed no more than a fairy. It was almost comical watching the lady try and hang on as a small child stood in front of the trailer brandishing a carrot in the hope it would change the little chestnut pony's mind.

I pulled my bag close, worrying about Kalila and Lubna being pulled around by Chintzy and flicked my eyes back to the big lorry in front of me. As soon as the ramp hit the floor Kalila calmly walked up the ramp of the horse lorry with Chintzy happily following her until they reached a big fat haynet stuffed full at the tie-up point.

Kalila tied her pony up, put the barriers up and popped the ramp up with ease that showed she had done it a hundred times before. Working as a team that didn't need words, Lubna and Kalila pushed the ramp-up and once slotted up pulled a bolt into place. I turned back to see the chestnut pony was still pulling the lady around the car park stopping only to stand on its back legs.

As Kalila and I climbed up into the passenger side of the lorry I said "Wow, Chintzy loads too easy." Kalila smiled and said "Not as easy as yours" as she glanced at my backpack with Tiny inside.

On the journey home, we were happy-tired. All our energy from this morning's horse show left us still on a high but too tired to have the same butterflies we had on the way there. Lubna handed us a huge bag of snacks and we tucked in.

Nineteen

Chapter 19

Waking up was strange this morning. Mum wasn't rushing and panicking. For the first time ever, I came down to see her at the kitchen table sipping a coffee instead of her cajoling me out of bed like a whirlwind. The calmness and not rushing were concerning.

"Morning mum" I smiled at her, sensing her worry and sadness.

"Hey, can you whip yourself up some breakfast? I'm having a think with my morning coffee today" Mum's lack of urgency was spooky.

"Yeah, of course. I'll grab some porridge then get my uniform on for school," I told her, trying to take care of myself so she wouldn't have to worry about me. I thought about asking her what would happen now, if she still had to go to work and finish up her notice or if she was finished as of now but I didn't want to stress her. I suppose her lack of movement answered my question.

"The car is still broken, can you walk yourself to school today, or get the school bus?" Mum asked

"Yeah" I answered even though I wanted to try and get a day off. I knew that being around Mum when she was this sad isn't ideal.

It turned out that this was our new morning routine. Mum sipping a coffee and me getting myself to school for the next few days.

Life would have lost its sparkle if it wasn't for having Tiny with me as a pocket-sized best friend.

There were no articles in my magazines on how to keep a hamster sized pony safe at times that I couldn't hold her. It didn't tell me where to put Tiny when I was in PE at school, or having a bath myself, and making sure she didn't escape into the classroom now Rebecca wasn't there to help me. I did work things out though and the detention was working out well. Being allowed to sit in a class-room alone at break times meant that I could pull Tiny out and play knowing the teachers' clackity heels would always warn me when they were coming.

Uncle Joe would be at my house already sitting with mum when I came in, helping make the tea as she sat chatting with him about jobs she should apply for.

The recycling bin overflowed, the dishes piled up in the sink and Mum didn't seem to cheer up so Tiny was the most welcome of distractions. Tiny became used to living with me rather than in her field. Tiny had a little box that I put her in now at bedtime so we had no more mishaps with escaping, and I would read to her at night in bed. I would sneak handfuls of grass into my pockets on the way to school and back and let Tiny chew on them.

Twenty

Chapter 20

"Mum, can I go straight to the stables after the yard today to see Kalila?" I asked.

Mum was still too busy worrying about paying bills and getting a job and feeling upset that her work had fired her. At least once a day I would overhear her tell someone "The extra amount I could have recycled for a few more pounds, all they care about is the money...sacked from a recycling plant for being too good at recycling" but nobody ever gave her a reply that stopped her constantly mulling over it.

I had butterflies in my tummy all day waiting for Uncle Joe to come and collect me. Erin stamped on my bag but her nonsense didn't worry me as I had Tiny safely in a little bum bag that I had taken to wearing under my jumper. Any second I could be alone, I could pop Tiny out. My lunchbox with holes fitted in it perfectly to make sure that she was never crushed. I put my hand up to ask to go to the bathroom a lot, but I was always told yes so got plenty of pony breaks, plus being in detention was such a pleasure as it meant being able to spend time with Tiny.

When Uncle Joe dropped me at the yard, I didn't wait to watch him pull away. I ran straight in to see if Kalila was with Chintzy.

She had a shiny and pristine saddle next to a similarly clean Chintzy. "Hey, have you got Tiny and your machine?" She greeted me with a big grin.

"Defo and I wanted to see if you fancied going for a ride together?"

"Ok, can you carry Tiny till we are over the first hill, so nobody sees you making her bigger? Holly might notice an extra pony kicking about the place?"

"Good idea, we don't want her thinking she has an extra pony and popping Tiny into one of the riding lessons with a random kid" I smiled.

I went into Kalila's stable and popped Tiny out onto the nice thick straw bed and sat down beside her. As Kalila began to tack up I popped Tiny's stuff out and got her ready at the same time, my tongue staying in my mouth now I knew what I was doing. I must have had the hang of it as we were ready to go at the same time - either that or it was easier to get a very small pony ready.

Kalila led Chintzy out of the stable to the big mounting block outside and climbed aboard. We smiled at Holly as we passed her and Kalila told her "See you soon, I've got Lilly walking with me today, so I might be a bit longer".

I kept marching beside her as Holly nodded and we made our way up the first hill. The excitement flowing through me gave me the energy to stride quickly up the hill and once we reached the peak the walking became easier. "I'm having to trot to keep up with you," she said as she squeezed her pony and popped into a trot forward.

I kept my pace and said, "I just want to get down this hill, behind the ditch before I make Tiny riding size."

I found my spot with a bush beside a fallen down tree trunk and Kalila brought Chintzy to a halt. Kalila let go of the reins so Chintzy could reach the grass and she immediately started munching on the long lush ungrazed grass. "That's her handbrake, she won't move a muscle now. Let's do it!".

I popped Tiny out onto the tree trunk and set up my machine. The familiar noises kicked in and suddenly Tiny was full size, but the tree trunk was giant. I grabbed some branches hanging off the side and started to climb.

"I'll come up the tree roots at the bottom and meet you up there Kalila called". Tiny stood watching me try and climb up as fast as I could, and the birds continued their song as though seeing random objects suddenly grow as part of their everyday world. I made sure my backpack was tight on my shoulders so I didn't drop it with my machine inside while I made my way to the top.

"I was hoping to use the tree trunk to mount from," I called to Kalila who was nearly caught up with me having made it along the roots onto the main stump. "That's ok", she said as she swung her legs round to the same side and popped off Chintzy. "Here, take a leggie up," she told me cupping her hands and wrapping them around the front of my ankle as she boosted me into the air. I got on board and was still fumbling around getting my feet back into the stirrups whilst Kalila had already effortlessly popped back onto Chintzy.

"Yaay...happy hacking time," she said as Tiny followed behind Chintzy and we found our way back to the oversized tree stump.

"Do you think anyone might notice what happened to the tree?" I asked

Kalila laughed "Yeah they might just not notice the world's biggest tree trunk suddenly appeared today, but their first guess is never gonna be that it had anything to do with us."

The sun was in the sky so that it would look warm in a photo but when you're in it you feel the chill. The hills were rolling and green with winding paths running all over the place and I was glad to have someone who knew the way and had ridden this before. We brought the horses up so that they were next to each other and rode side by side blethering, laughing, and joking as we went. Feeling Tiny sway as she walked was glorious and I was loving every moment of my dream day out. We decided to trot for a while, and I listened to the hoof beats, albeit quieter when on the grassy hill, still a sound to make my heart beat faster. "Fancy a canter up the hill?" Kalila asked. I felt I could manage anything on Tiny and nodded eagerly. I didn't even have to ask Tiny to canter once Chintzy sprang into a floaty canter, Tiny just followed along with a rhythmic speed. I felt the power underneath me from Tiny's strong legs extending and gathering back together, speeding away up the hill. At the top of the hill, I pulled the reins and asked Tiny to slow down back to a trot and she immediately came back down to her marching beat before falling into a walk beside Chintzy. The exhilaration of the canter stayed with me long after we had slowed down to wander in and out of the stream making big splooshy splashy noises with their hooves.

We wandered along the stream and once I started feeling a little braver, we jumped over the stream in the narrower bits. Kalila jumped some of the wider riverbanks and then jumped back towards me. My smile was so big the sides of my mouth were pointed at my ears. We stopped to let the ponies graze some of the lush grass, and as Tiny lowered her head to guzzle, I said "Look, I've got a handbrake now too!"

I stopped the cantering when it was time to head back, wanting to take as long as I could to lap up every moment of joy. I wanted the wander home to take forever, the contentment that followed the excitement of the cantering thrills. I copied Kalila and stopped keeping contact with my hands and gave Tiny a long rein as she enjoyed daundering back. I pulled Tiny to a halt then realised I should ride up the tree again so that I wouldn't be leaving the countryside in all sizes of disarray behind me. It might be a little odd and suspicious after all the work that I had done on keeping Tiny secret.

Tiny made her way up the roots of the fallen down tree until we were back up on top of it and Chintzy stood beside it. "Can you make Chintzy small so I can bring her home to my bedroom with me?" Kalila asked as she watched me pull my backpack off and set up the machine to shrink down Tiny.

"I'm not sure. Won't Holly notice she's missing though?" I asked

"Hmmm, she might just think I'm out at a show, though. Go on, you get to take your pony home all the time"

"I'm really worried about getting caught though. If I start shrinking loads of ponies I'm more likely to get caught."

Kalila looked disappointed and I felt guilty. I didn't want to let her down but I don't think she understood that any other way of owning a pony was never going to happen for me.

"How about we do it one night when we have a sleepover or something and that way, I can make sure she is big again for the next day and is back in her stable before anyone notices?"

Kalila's normal chattiness stopped as she looked a bit annoyed and she didn't speak as I put Tiny in my pocket and ran to keep up with her and Chintzy.

She seemed to forget she was annoyed with me by the time we got back to the stables with me walking beside her and said "I'll ask my mum for that sleepover next weekend. It was great having a hacking partner today".

Kalila was just untacking and telling me where to take the handfuls of hay from Tiny to have at home and some pony nuts for supper when Holly came in.

"You must be tired of walking for hours with Kalila and Chintzy," Holly said to me. Tired and saddle sore I thought as my leg muscles ached. "I loved it. It was so pretty out there" I told her.

When bedtime came, I closed my eyes and pictured all the things I had seen and done on my ride. The views of the Scottish hills, the trees as we cantered up to them, the sounds of the water as we rode through it, the feel of butterflies when we sped up and my warm thoughts led me to a deep slumber.

Twenty-One

Chapter 21

When the morning arrived, I slept longer than usual but I had a great plan. I picked Tiny up, and still in my pyjamas took her out to graze for a while in the garden. I made a little head collar from some binder twine used to hold the bales together that had come with the hay Kalila had given me.

Tiny loved munching outside like a real horse and as she was grazing, I began to wonder how I could Tiny proof a small part of the garden so I could maybe give her some turn out. I sat in my pyjamas on the grass. Such a sweet pony but she did deserve more, to get a herd her own size to hang out with. My mind wandered if it would be easier to get lots of ponies somehow and shrink them down for Tiny to play with or make Tiny big and put her with some regular sized ponies. As I was deep in my thoughts I saw Mum out the corner of my eye, over by the hedge.

"Lilly, what are you doing out here in your pyjamas?" I opened my mouth to answer her but before I could think of a lie to tell her she waved a letter at me and said, "And the school has let me know you have been up to all sorts and keeping it from me." Mum walked closer and I panicked, she was close enough to see Tiny and only her rage seemed to have stopped her from noticing so far. "Mum wait,

I'm coming, I'm coming!" I said sneaking Tiny under my pyjama top and running into the house in front of her. "I'm just going to the loo, upset tummy!" I shouted as I ran ahead and hid Tiny in her case in my backpack in the hall before running upstairs to the bathroom.

I felt dread at the trouble I was in with Mum with equal measures of relief that she hadn't spotted Tiny. I didn't think I would be allowed any sleepovers or days out at the riding school ever again. I wasn't even dressed and I felt this was going to be one of those telling offs that lasted all day.

I steeled myself to go and deal with it and flushed the toilet to make mum think I had really been in the bathroom.

I walked down the stairs as quickly as I could thinking of as many excuses as I could about why I hadn't told her about the detention.

Mum was sitting in the living room with her face red and furious to match her red eyes from the last few days. "So, you've been getting into fights at school, then hiding detentions from me?." she shouted.

"Mum, I wasn't fighting and....." but she cut me off.

"Don't you think I have enough problems? Do you think getting in a fight with anyone is ever the answer to anything? Then keeping it from me. What else have you been hiding from me?" Mum was in full rant mode now and her words went on and on in one long angry loud tone. There wasn't any stopping her when she was this way. The best way to calm her down was to shut up and let it pass, any arguing back just made things worse.

"Lilly, you have been up to something. I can just tell. I want to know everything. I want the slips the school has been sending home for you out of your bag this second". She whizzed across the room to the hall and in a heartbeat, she had my backpack in her hand.

I was terrified she would throw it down but even more terrifying was what actually happened. She continued shouting and ranting at me as she unzipped my bag and pulled out the box containing Tiny. "This has been destroyed with holes in it. Why would you even do that? I can't afford a new one and now you're wrecking your stuff and getting in fights!" she said, waving the lunchbox around as she yelled.

I burst into tears and yelled "Mum no, stop it" but she kept going and in a fit of rage, she shouted "Well this lunch box is just rubbish now anyway" and threw it hard on the floor. "Noooooooo," I shouted back and grabbed the lunchbox from the ground and tried to run past mum to get up the stairs with my precious Tiny.

My heart was pounding terrified that Tiny had been hurt. Tiny began whinnying and a banging came from inside the box as her little hooves banged against the side. Mum snatched the box back from me on hearing the banging and slowly began to open the lid and peered inside.

When mum's eyes fell on Tiny, she looked confused. So confused there was no room for anger in her head anymore. The miracle of her returning quickly to calm had arrived but been replaced by the disaster of her discovering my secret.

"Lilly, what on earth is this?"

"Mum, this is Tiny. Tiny is a pony, but extremely small"

"But you don't get ponies this size," she said, staring wide-eyed at Tiny, her voice low and quiet again. "How?"

The room stayed silent awhile as Mum gently picked Tiny out of the box. My voice came out squeaky when I finally tried to explain, "Natasha and Erin were picking on me, Mum. I didn't fight. I liked detention because I got peace from them. And this is Tiny and Tiny is my pony. I want to keep her and she doesn't cost anything to keep and I will be responsible and look after her."

"How?" Mum asked again slowly as though she hadn't heard a word. Her eyes were still agape, staring at Tiny as she held her in her hand.

I fetched a carrot stick from the fridge and came back and said to Mum, "Look at this, sit next to me" as I folded my legs and sat on the floor. Mum's mouth stayed wide and her eyes didn't come off Tiny as she lowered herself to the floor. I placed Tiny and the carrot on the floor and Tiny started to munch away on the carrot. "It's real," Mum whispered. "How did you find it?"

I knew honesty was going to get me further and there was no talking myself out of this one. "Do you remember the farmer was going to shoot the last pony that was left in the field? He did say I could have it if I wanted it?"

"Hmmmmmmmmm," mum replied, so I assumed she was now listening and continued.

"And in Uncle Joe's unfinished projects he had a minimising microscope. He thought it would never work so he said if I could fix it, I could keep it. I suppose he didn't realise it would ever work. Well, that's how I managed to make the pony small so I could keep it."

"Lilly, this is amazing, this is so much bigger than a tiny pony, or a full-size pony, any pony, you know what I mean."

"Yeah, I know I studied inventions that were weaponised at school. That's why we need to not tell anyone," I said.

She stood up and picked up her phone and started to video call Uncle Joe. "Mum, will you make me give it back? I know I can't keep Tiny if she is full size". I asked her. As Uncle Joe answered mum put Tiny on the screen and showed him. "What's this, some special effect?" he laughed when he answered before he continued "I love the filters you get on video calls these days."

"Lilly got your machine working. This is the pony the farmer wanted to shoot. He's been living in her bag apparently."

"Wow, that's genius" Uncle Joe said "How did you fix it?" he asked. The engineer in Uncle missed the point. The fact a mini pony was running around seemed not so much to concern him as the mechanics of the machine now working.

"My glasses and my old watch battery," I told him.

Mum asked him, "Can we make another? Joe, if this works, can you imagine the recycling business of my own I could run, I could just make the waste smaller and smaller until what was a million tonnes is a gram before it goes to the landfill. We could make millions by saving the planet."

Joe seemed much less phased than Mum. "I bagsy being the engineering consultant. I can maintain the machine on my better days. Once Lilly trains me since she's the one that got it going in the end" he laughed.

"But no, if you use the machine for your business and recycling then I won't be able to make Tiny big again when she needs it, and we won't be able to keep her full size" I panicked.

"I don't think it's fair to keep a pony all shrunk down, without other horse friends. Your bedroom isn't the right environment. I think we should make a call to the riding school and see if there is a stable free. Tiny needs a normal pony life," Mum said to my surprise.

Uncle Joe piped up, "I can afford the first couple of months' livery until the business is off the ground, I think your Mum's right about keeping a pony in y'2our bedroom, but I think you're right about not telling anyone about the technology."

Mum was talking urgently now. "I think the business is a great idea, I'm deadly serious. And of course, we could afford a pony if I had my own recycling business. But Joe, this is your machine?"

Uncle Joe answered "Look, this is the answer to so many problems. You keep this machine and start the business. I am happy to be on the payroll as a consultant for keeping it working and maintain it. I might manage to make another and go travelling while doing some charity work, using it as a maximising telescope to solve food shortages. I could do that wherever needed and as a consultant, I can video call to sort anything. We can find a way of working out the practicalities. The recycling business you want to set up needs done so you go for that."

So, keeping Tiny, full-sized, at the riding school, means that dreams genuinely do come true.

"You're still going to be apologising at school for causing so much trouble," Mum brought me back to reality with a thump. But apologising seemed more bearable with a pony to come home to every day.

Twenty-Two

Chapter 22

I stood in the stable next to Chintzy, running my lovely new brushes from my posh fancy grooming kit over a super shiny black coat.

I picked up my new mobile phone and looked at the texts and saw one from Kalila saying, "Yeah, let's do the big jumps today, be over in five."

I put it back in my pocket and kept grooming away, singing as I groomed.

Holly came into the barn and said, "Are you okay there Lilly? You seem to have taken to pony ownership like a duck to water."

"Yeah, it's what I always wanted. I feel so lucky."

"Do you want me to send one of the helpers to muck out for you when you're riding later? I have Natasha looking for a job."

"No, that's nice of you but I quite enjoy doing it myself."

"She's well looked after, that's for sure. Is your Uncle Joe coming to pick you up later? I would love to have someone look at the outside tap later."

"He's here somewhere. He dropped me off, but he's just building up my new wheelbarrow. I'll let him know you're looking for him when he appears," I told her.

As though he could sense it, as soon as Holly left, Uncle Joe appeared.

"You scored big time, you know. Having the stable next to your friend, having me still chauffeur you...all your nice stuff! I'll have to let you fix my machines more often."

He smiled.

"Shhhhh!" I told him, smiling back. He was right.

"Holly was looking for you to fix the tap," I remembered.

"I'm gonna sneak by her."

Uncle Joe loved working for Mum at her new business. He kept recycling machines working, and Mum let him work around when he wasn't well.

"I love fixing things, but today, I just wanna hang with ponies and enjoy my day off," he said as he went to leave.

I loved this new life.

CPSIA information can be obtained
at www.ICGtesting.com
Printed in the USA
BVHW080819230522
637793BV00002B/69